Ronald A. Rowbottom is retired after a career of forty-seven years in the environmental health and safety field which has allowed him to see much of the world. He holds a jurist doctorate degree focused on environmental and social law from the University of Denver, Sturm College of Law, Denver, Colorado. Ron now has the time to write, having published Flights of Poetry in 2017. He is writing a series of crime mystery novels based on the character Detective Tom Grant based in London, Ontario, Canada.

As always, this novel is dedicated to my friend and companion of forty nine years, Teddy Rowbottom. You have stood by me throughout all of our life's journey and been the anchor for our daughter and two sons. I also dedicate this to my two outstanding adult grandchildren, Kobe and Trinity.

This is also dedicated to all those individuals and groups working to aid people who are suffering from drug addiction and bullying.

The Case of the Deadly Séance

A Detective Tom Grant Investigation

Ronald A. Rowbottom

Bennett books may be ordered through booksellers or by contacting:

Bennett Media and Marketing
1603 Capitol Ave., Suite 310 A233
Cheyenne, WY 82001
www.thebennettmediaandmarketing.com
Phone: 1-307-202-9292

ISBN: 978-1-957114-30-9 (paperback)
ISBN: 978-1-957114-29-3 (eBook)

Printed in the United States of America

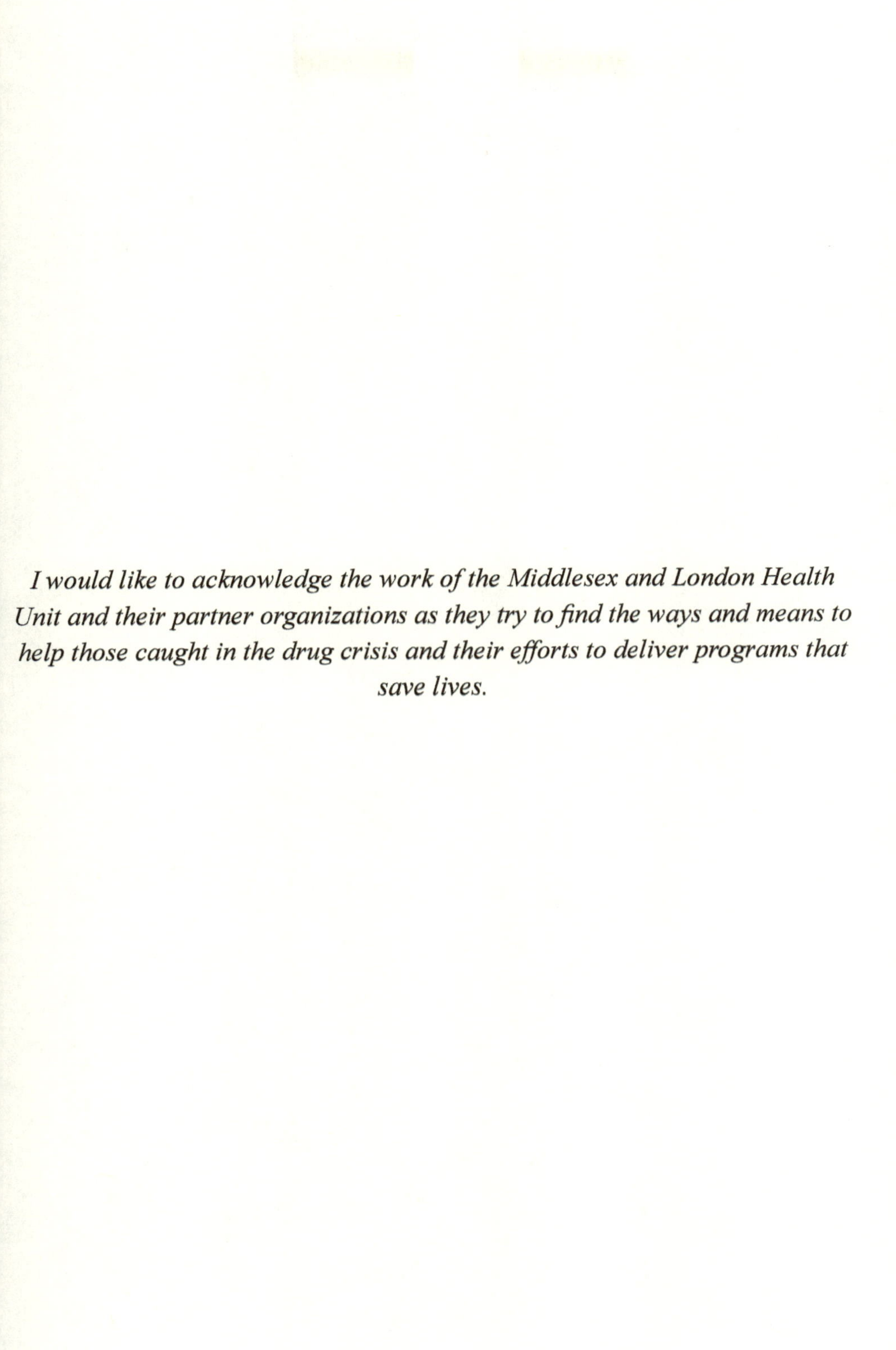

I would like to acknowledge the work of the Middlesex and London Health Unit and their partner organizations as they try to find the ways and means to help those caught in the drug crisis and their efforts to deliver programs that save lives.

RONALD A. ROWBOTTOM

CHAPTER 1:
WEEK EIGHT

The Shepherds lived in a comfortable home located on Jarvis Street just off Springbank Drive in London, Ontario. The street was a quiet, mature maple tree lined dead end street that did not seem like the place for anything out of the ordinary to happen.

Debbie Shepherd was 16 years old, a good student but she was not interested in athletics. Her mousy brown hair and stocky build allowed her to blend into the woodwork at school. She was never the class leader or even much noticed by most of the other students except the ones who saw her as fair game for bullying. Debbie was targeted as an individual that other students could tease and make fun of both online and in person.

Her classmates had tormented her through social media online with fat comments and joke postings. In person, it was just as bad as she was routinely subjected to mean remarks, hurtful illustrations, and altered photographs posted on school bulletin boards.

Her only friend had been Mary Summers, another girl much like her, indistinguishable in the crowd of their fellow classmates except to those individuals who made themselves feel superior by belittling others. The two of them had bonded and commiserated in their isolation until last summer when Mary's family moved to another city leaving Debbie alone in her world.

Slowly, she had sunk into depression and loneliness until one fall morning Debbie cried quietly as she sat at the small desk in the corner of her bedroom. Her hands placed gently on the Ouija board in front of her.

"Please I want to speak with my grandmother," she whispered as she rested her hands on the pointer.

Her grandmother had been the one person that Debbie felt she could turn to and that had accepted and loved her unconditionally. Last month, her grandmother had passed away leaving her feeling that she was totally alone. She felt abandoned and afraid.

Slowly, she felt her hands begin to move on top of the pointer as she sat expectantly hoping for a response.

"Grandma, I wish I could be with you," she sobbed.

A voice spoke gently behind her, "That can be arranged," and then everything went black.

A small flame flickered to life near the corner of the room next to the curtains on the window and grew quickly into a blaze filling the room with smoke.

Debbie could not hear the scream of the smoke detector as it blared in the growing light.

Monday September the 10th, the buzzing of the alarm clock split the morning silence jolting Detective Tom Grant awake. He slammed his hand against the clock radio to silence the noise and looked at his sleeping wife, curled under the sheets in their king size bed.

At age 64, Tom was finding it harder and harder to come to life at the start of a new workday as he had just a few years ago. His mind had begun to accept the idea of retiring in a few months after 43 years on the London Police Force.

Tom would turn 65 years old on November the third, and in preparation he had applied for this Canada Pension Plan retirement pension to start the month after he met that age. Officially, he would be retired as of December the first but he would actually finish working on November the second. The balance of the month of November was unused vacation and accumulated sick time.

His job had been fulfilling and he felt he made a difference, but he was getting tired and his body ached more than it used to.

"It's time for you to actually retire when you turn 65," Ann had told him. Tom had agreed even though he secretly knew that it was going to turn not only his life upside down but would also turn his wife's, Ann's, life upside down.

Both had their long-established routines, his with the police force and hers as a homemaker with all the activities outside the home that she took part in.

Tom could not envision himself as a stay at home retiree, watching TV and complaining about the weather, but he really didn't know what he was going to do when that day finally arrived.

He sighed and rolled out of the bed and headed into the shower to get ready for day number thirty-nine of the last thirty-nine workdays he had left.

He stared at his reflection in the bathroom mirror. His grey hair was still full except for the shrinking hairline. He chuckled as he remembered the question his youngest son had asked him yesterday when the family had gathered for Sunday dinner.

"Dad, what do you call a line of rabbits hopping backwards?"

When Tom had admitted he did not have an answer, his son had rubbed his hand across Tom's forehead, "A receding hair line."

The thought of endless days of bad puns and inactivity made him wonder if he was really doing the right thing by retiring.

After he shaved and dressed in his standard suit for work, he brushed off the cobwebs in his mind and reminded himself that retirement would be as good or bad as he chose to make it.

Tom arrived at Police Headquarters located at 601 Dundas Street at 8:00 a.m. and went to his office in the Criminal Investigation Division, Major Crimes Section.

Again, he was reminded of his upcoming retirement when he went to grab a cup of coffee from the break room. The other members of the department had switched out his old coffee mug last week with a new one that stated, *RETIRED, Goodbye Tension, Hello Pension!*

He had asked where his old familiar coffee mug was, but everyone joked that it was all part of the process of change. He had smiled but deep down he really wasn't happy with the subtle changes in his routine that everyone was creating. He knew it was all meant in fun but it just highlighted the inevitable.

Tom settled into his desk chair and studied the pictures he kept on his office walls as he sipped his coffee.

He liked viewing things that displayed the history of the force, it made him feel connected and grounded.

The central framed photograph on the wall was the first police station located in the rear of the then new city hall on Richmond Street overlooking Covent Garden's Market in 1855 for the newly established London Police Force.

The 1911 photograph next to it was taken of the police force in front of the Carling Street Station.

1 Museum London Archives

The photo on the other side showed that in 1937, the police force moved to a new location, the 1970 King Street Station. At that time, the building was heralded as:

The
London,
Ontario,
Police
Administration
Building
is one of the
most
modern
on this
continent

2 Museum London Archives
3 Museum London Archives

Tom had started his career on the force in 1975 just after the London Police Services relocated to its current headquarters located at 601 Dundas Street, built in 1974 at the site of the former Globe Gasket Company.

Back then, members of the police services made comments about the former occupants of the site and how they made caskets for the deceased and the police services were in the business of trying to prevent them from getting new customers.

The final plaque on the wall displayed the London Police Services Crest and Motto: Facta Non Verba – Deeds Not Words.

Even after being a member of the force for 43 years, Tom still felt a surge of pride when he considered the history of the force and his role in helping to fulfill that motto.

He had just finished his moments of contemplation and emptied his coffee cup when his desk phone rang.

There had been a fire this morning at a home on Jarvis Street, just off Springbank Road close to Springbank Park, and a young girl had been found dead.

Major Crimes Investigations Unit was being requested to attend at the scene.

Tom collected his junior partner, Brad Logan, from the detective's bullpen and advised him of the call. He watched Brad as he gathered up his suit coat and cell phone and felt the pang of apprehension. Brad was new to the major crimes division having been promoted just six months ago. The duty officer had assigned Brad to Tom so that he could mentor and advise him. It was felt that rookie detective Logan could learn the ropes from Tom before retirement would take that experience away from the department. Tom realized that it was meant as a compliment, but it just kept the reality of his leaving forefront in his mind.

"What's the details?" Brad queried as they headed out the door towards their parked vehicle.

"All I know is that there was a fire and a teenage girl died in the blaze."

"Doesn't sound like a case for major crimes based on that description."

"Maybe but until we get there we will not know why we are being called, so it's best to not speculate and just keep an open mind till we see the scene."

The two drove in silence down Adelaide Street and turned right on Horton Street. Jarvis Street was just a 15-minute drive from the station following Horton to Springbank and turning left on Jarvis.

Policing the City of London did not entail long drives as it is relatively compact, covering a space of 420 square kilometers with a population of three hundred and eighty-four thousand residents within the city limits.

When Tom had started with the force, the city was just under two hundred and fifty thousand residents, and even though the population had grown during his career, it still had the feel of the small city that he knew and loved.

His mind drifted back to his earlier days, and he envisioned the changes that have taken place over the years. The downtown still maintained the character of a downtown business core with narrow streets that created problems for on-street parking. The reality of a busy freight and passenger train track cut the city in half. Trains ran through the downtown creating routine traffic jams when trains rolled through. City council had been trying over the years to come up with ways to alleviate the concern as part of a Bus Rapid Transit overhaul within the city, but the railroad crossings were not able to be moved and the building of rail overpasses over the majority of street crossings was not feasible. At one point, the city council had even considered constructing a vehicle tunnel to go under the Richmond Street railroad crossing which affected the main downtown, but the cost and engineering concerns for the stores and churches along the route proved to be unfeasible.

Tom was jolted back to the present when Brad turned off Springbank onto the short street of Jarvis.

It was a quiet dead end neighborhood of family homes that had been built in the '70s with well-maintained houses and yards. The type of neighborhood where everyone knew each other and kids grew up feeling safe.

The front of the last house on the street was cordoned off with yellow barrier tape, and the fire trucks had left except for the assistant deputy chief's response vehicle which was parked on the street. A cruiser stood guard at the entrance with its flashing red and blue lights alerting the neighbors that something had gone terribly wrong.

Tom noted the London Regional Coroner's van in the driveway which meant the coroner's office was waiting for their arrival before removing the body, a fact that left him wondering if this was more than a simple fire fatality.

The assistant deputy fire chief met them at the front door. "What have we got?" Brad queried.

"The fire was reported at 7:15 this morning when the alarm monitoring company notified us of an alarm.

"The home was built in 1974 but the current owners had installed an upgraded alarm and home fire suppression sprinkler system a few years ago. The fire had been contained to a section of the victim's bedroom by the sprinklers so that when we arrived it was basically extinguished.

"That area of the bedroom experienced the most extensive damage but the balance of the home was subject to moderate smoke and water affects. Initial review of the fire scene indicates the use of an accelerant to start the blaze in the area of the floor, beside the bed and curtains. We have concluded that this is a suspicious fire and have requested the Forensic Unit to perform an arson analysis, but basically the scene now belongs to you."

"Thanks," Tom replied, "Give us a copy of your final report when it is ready."

The officer on duty at the door directed Tom and Brad to the rear of the home where the bedroom in question was located.

The home was neat and orderly, not fancy by any standards, but functional and undisturbed except for the acrid odor of smoke that permeated the rooms.

Tom entered the bedroom and surveyed the scene from the doorway. The corner of the room beside the bed was badly burned including the wall and curtains. On the other side of the room, a teenage girl was slumped face down over a small metal desk. The fire had been contained by the sprinklers so that the body showed little affects from the fire except for some blistering that was visible on her arms and face caused by the heat.

The regional coroner greeted the detectives and extended her hand to shake Tom's and Brad's.

"This is a messy business," she remarked. "We notified major crimes because of the circumstance. The sprinklers kept the fire from engulfing the whole area which left the body basically intact. The girl was struck from behind which, based on the injury, would have rendered her unconscious but does not look severe enough to cause death. My assumption is that she died from smoke inhalation, but I will not be able to confirm till the autopsy."

"The quick action of the sprinklers was not sufficient to prevent the smoke build up?" Brad questioned.

"Had her body fell to the floor it may have been but since she was slumped onto the desk the height of her head allowed for the buildup of smoke from the roof downwards.

"Most fire deaths are not caused by burns, but by smoke inhalation. Even when a victim is awake often times smoke incapacitates so quickly that people are overcome and cannot make it to an otherwise accessible exit. The synthetic materials commonplace in today's homes produce especially dangerous substance. Smoke particles can be so small they penetrate the respiratory system's protective filters and lodge in the lungs. Carbon monoxide, CO, can be deadly even in small quantities as it replaces the oxygen in the blood. Hydrogen cyanide results from the burning of plastics and vinyl materials and produces phosgene when burned.

"Once I have the autopsy results, I can narrow down the substances, but it will still likely lead to the initial conclusion of respiratory failure from smoke inhalation."

Tom thanked the coroner and asked her to keep them posted of any developments as he released the body to the coroner.

"What's next?" Brad asked.

"As this is now a suspected homicide, let's talk to the officer on duty who arrived first and see if the department's Forensics Identification Unit have come up with anything concrete yet regarding intruder entry, etc."

Pete Sloan was the lead forensic unit investigator on the scene, and he had arrived a short time before Tom and Brad.

"Have you found anything at this point?" Tom asked after locating Pete in the kitchen of the home.

"The scratch marks on the rear door indicate that someone used a small pry bar to break open the lock. The security alarm was disengaged which means either the alarm had not been activated or the intruder knew the code. We are collecting evidence, but it will take time to sort out what is normally here versus what may have been left by the intruder.

"We did find a muddy footprint on the back step and the damp grass indicates that the sprinklers were on earlier. This may provide us route of access for the intruder across the back lawn from the small bush area behind the property. Probably exited the same way. We are searching the bush lot to see if we can find anything more on that front, and we have taken an imprint and photograph of the boot print.

"Initial indications point to the fact the intruder was not at the home for a random burglary but was very direct in the intent to enter the home and kill the girl. It appears to be very deliberate and planned based on the information gathered so far."

Tom pondered this in his mind as the case now appeared to move from a fire accident victim to a homicide to pre-meditated murder. He silently wondered if the remaining fifty-two days before his retirement would allow him to solve this case or if he would be leaving the force with work left undone.

Brad broke into his contemplation by asking if he would share his thoughts.

"Not a whole lot to share at this point. Let's go back to the station and see if the parents have been contacted. We need to talk with them about some inconsistencies such as the disabled security alarm, etc."

"I don't relish that task," Brad mused. "Having to be told they just lost their daughter and all."

"It comes with the job," Tom replied.

They drove back the short distance to the station and then proceeded to look up background information on Frank and Elizabeth Shepherd, Deborah's parents.

Frank was a tenured professor of economics at the University of Western Ontario in London.

Tom researched information on Western University.

The institution was founded on March 7th, 1878. Western's co-educational student body of over 24,000 represents 107 countries and Western scholars have established research and education collaborations and partnerships in every continent. Notable alumni include government officials, academics, business leaders, Nobel Laureates, Rhodes Scholars, and distinguished fellows.

Frank Shepherd was listed as a respected professor at the university for over 20 years with no criminal record, citations, or complaints on file.

Elizabeth Shepherd was employed as a registered nurse at Parkwood Rehabilitation Institute in London.

Parkwood, part of St. Joseph's Health Care Network in London, is described as 'a vibrant academic health care community that is collaborating in physical and mental health care, teaching and research and advancing the understanding that conditions of the body and mind go hand-in-hand.' Parkwood's description noted that the facility specialized in care, recovery, and rehabilitation.

Like her husband Frank, Elizabeth had no criminal record, citations, or complaints on file.

Records noted the Elizabeth and Frank were married in 2000, the Shepherds had purchased the home on Jarvis Street in 2001, shortly before their daughter was born. Deborah was their only child.

Tom made a note to consider if there were any possible connections to the university or rehabilitation center that could have triggered someone to have undertaken revenge against either of the parents. He needed to consider if anyone had expressed anger or feelings of perceived harm against the Shepherds due to any interaction with a student, patient, or family member at either institution.

He knew this would be a long shot, but all possibilities needed to be considered.

In addition, they needed to get more details about Debbie's school life, activities, friends, etc.

Brad entered Tom's office and advised him that the mother, Elizabeth was in the interview room and that the father was on his way from the university. They had been contacted in person by uniformed officers and asked to come to the station but not advised about the fire or their daughter at this point.

"Did either one seem to be aware of what happened this morning at their home?" Tom queried.

"Not based on the current state of Mrs. Shepherd. She appears concerned about being asked to the station but not emotionally upset."

"Interesting," Tom mused, "Obviously none of the neighbors at the scene either knew them well enough or were able to contact them in regard to the activity that was taking place at their home."

Tom and Brad entered the interview room and introduced themselves to Elizabeth Shepherd. She was a lady in her late thirties or early forties, around 1.7 meters in height, blonde hair, and striking blue eyes. She was dressed in pale blue nurses' scrubs. Her apprehension was clearly visible as she stood and shook the detective's hands.

"I am not sure why you had me come here. Is this something to do with Parkwood or a patient?" she asked. "Everyone in the health care industry has been on edge since the revelation and conviction of Nurse Wettlaufer recently."

Tom remembered the Wettlaufer case well. Elizabeth Wettlaufer was a former nurse that had pleaded guilty and been convicted of killing eight elderly residents, and the attempted murder of four others while in her care at Ontario nursing homes in Woodstock, Paris and London as well as private home care between 2007 and 2016.

It had been a case that shocked the public and the Ministry of Health regarding the monitoring of nursing homes and had left the Ontario College of Nurses struggling with the negative perception that the case had cast over the nursing profession.

In 2017, the Long-Term Care Homes Public Inquiry had been established by an Order in Council by the provincial government to determine how the events could occur and to make recommendations so that these tragedies could not happen in the future. The inquiry had recently concluded public hearings and was scheduled to release its final report in July 2019.

Tom assured her that they needed to talk to her and her husband on a separate matter that was not directly related to the Parkwood Institute.

At that moment, the door to the interview room opened and Frank Shepherd entered. Frank was in his mid-forties, dressed in a causal brown suede suit; he appeared the stereotypical professor of economics. His brown hair was cut short, with touches of grey.

Frank stared confused at his wife sitting at the interview table before he moved over to stand beside her.

"Elizabeth what's happening?" he queried. "Why are my wife and I here?"

"Please sit down," Tom replied. "We have some questions we need to ask you both and we will explain shortly. Could you each tell us when you left your home this morning?"

Elizabeth stated that she had left for work at 6:00 a.m. for her shift at Parkwood and Frank stated he had left shortly after at 6:15 to go to the university.

"Was anyone else at home when you left?"

"Our teenage daughter Debbie was in her room getting ready to leave for school at 7:30."

"Was there anyone else in the home?"

"No," replied Frank. "What is going on, has there been some trouble at Debbie's school or at home?"

Tom braced himself for the inevitable as he replied.

"We regret to inform you that there was a fire this morning at your home and that your daughter was found deceased."

The look of absolute shock on both their faces was heart rending for Tom as he watched the shock change to pain.

Both the Shepherds broke down in disbelief, Elizabeth had her face buried into her husband's shoulder.

"How!" exclaimed Frank.

"It appears that someone broke into your home after you left and murdered your daughter before attempting to cover the crime by setting fire in her bedroom. The sprinkler system extinguished the fire, but your daughter was already gone.

"I know this is hard, but we need to ask you some additional questions so that we can catch whoever did this to your daughter.

"We understand Mr. Shepherd that you work at the university and Mrs. Shepherd at Parkwood Institute. Have either of you had issues at work with a student or patient in the past several months? Are you aware of anyone that may have expressed anger or threatened either of you or your family? Any problems that you are aware of at school with other students, teachers, etc. that were aimed at Debbie?"

Elizabeth appeared to be in shock, but she replied that she was not aware of any problems. Frank stated that he had not heard of any issues. He mentioned that Elizabeth's mother, Debbie's grandmother, had passed away recently and Debbie and she had been very close.

Elizabeth also mentioned that Debbie had lost her best friend this past summer when her family moved away to another town and Debbie had been upset.

Tom asked if they could provide a list of friends that Debbie may be associated with as well as the contact information for the friend who had moved.

The interview concluded with Tom offering to provide Elizabeth and Frank a ride to the home of a friend or family member as their home was still under investigation for the fire and as a crime scene.

Frank asked when they would be able to see their daughter and go back to their home. They wanted to let friends and family know before the news went out in the press.

Tom could see they were both still deep in denial and grief.

"Detective Logan will make arrangements to take you to where your daughter is and answer any other questions you have based on what we know at this time. I am deeply sorry for your loss," Tom consoled, "Detective Logan will be in contact with you regarding the list of names etc."

Brad walked the couple out to the main entrance, making arrangements to have them driven to the morgue to identify the body of their daughter.

Tom re-entered the interview room after confirming that the Shepherds were being tended to by uniformed officers.

He sat in front of the interview table and surveyed the room. The cream-colored blank walls struck him as stark and bland except for the one-way glass panel and the mounted surveillance camera that captured everything that occurred in this room. Over the years, he had sat in this room many times to confront suspects and question individuals.

It had never felt so cold and barren before as it did just now. Maybe it was the Shepherds or maybe it was his pending retirement, but Tom suddenly realized that this room was not one of things he would miss about this job when he retired.

He sighed realizing that his mind was actually starting to come to grips with the conclusion that he would soon not be a part of all this.

Tom returned to his desk and spent the balance of the day working through his thoughts and the mountain of paperwork that accumulated daily before he washed his stained coffee cup left from the start of the day. He reflected back over the routine start of this morning and the turn his day had taken. He gathered his jacket and headed home to his wife.

The next morning, Brad had visited the Shepherds and returned with the list of names of school friends and associates the Shepherds had provided. The Shepherds were not aware of anyone who had expressed anger or revenge against them or their daughter. Tom and Brad started working through the list, and in addition, they decided to visit Debbie's school and the administrators at Western University and Parkwood.

The first stop was Saunders Secondary School located on Viscount Road where Debbie had attended and currently enrolled in grade 11. The school was located less than four kilometers from Debbie's home across from the Westmount Mall off Wonderland Road.

Tom and Brad entered the principal's office. They advised the principal that they were investigating the homicide of Deborah Shepherd and asked for information regarding Debbie's school attendance and attitude. The principal advised that Debbie had been a bit of a loner at school and her only close friend that he was aware of had transferred before the start of the school year to the Town of Simcoe, Ontario some 100 kilometers from London.

The school counselor came into the office and shared her notes regarding Debbie. She stated that there had been some complaints about other students being mean towards Debbie, posting derogatory materials on the bulletin board and online. The family had not filed any formal complaints and the counselor advised that she had talked with Debbie to help her too to not take the bullying seriously. She felt it had simply been teenagers being teenagers and had not escalated the issue to the principal.

Brad asked if there were records of any students in particular who had been involved but the counselor did not have any specifics.

Tom advised them that they were going to investigate the reports more closely and would likely be back to interview specific students.

The principal stated that he would not be comfortable with the police interviewing any of the students at the school without parents being notified.

"No problem," Tom replied. "We will pull the kids in question out of school and take them down to the station when the time is right and advise their parents."

He thanked the principal and the counselor for their cooperation and stated they would like to talk to Debbie's teachers before they left.

The principal provided them with an empty classroom to use and had the secretary arrange for Debbie's homeroom teacher to meet them there.

Mr. Saunders was an older gentleman and had been teaching mathematics at the school for nearly 40 years. He was obviously uncomfortable being questioned by the police but said he would help any way he could. He had heard about the fire and suspected homicide in the papers the night before but was not aware that it was Deborah Shepherd who was involved.

"I thought it was possibly gang related when I heard the story or involved drugs, but I never would have connected this to the Shepherds. They had come in just last week for a parent teacher meeting to talk about Debbie's school progress. They were concerned about how she was feeling with the loss of her grandmother and her best friend.

"I told them that Debbie was withdrawn and shy but that had been her normal attitude in the two years that she has attended the school. Debbie was not a very outgoing person, kept to herself and didn't seem to make a lot of friends with the other students."

"Were you aware of any issue regarding bullying that was occurring with the other students?" asked Brad.

"Yes, I have seen some small things like items that were posted on the bulletin board. Nothing too extreme, just hand drawn pictures referring to Debbie's size and her being so shy and withdrawn. I caught one girl posting a picture and had a good talk with her about appropriateness and being kind to others."

"Can you provide us the name of that student?" Tom questioned.

"Nancy Graves, she is in Debbie's home room class. Nancy is one of the most popular students always hanging in a crowd and seemingly in the middle of everything."

Brad marked Nancy's name in his notebook noting that she was one of the students they would want to talk to in more detail.

Mr. Saunders stated that was about all he could add regarding Debbie's situation. He noted that this school year would be his last as he was retiring after the spring semester.

Tom winched internally wondering if every day there was going to be another reminder of his countdown to leaving the work he knew he loved.

I wonder what I am really going to do with myself in two more months, he mentally questioned himself.

"What's eating you?" Brad asked after Saunders left, "You looked rather deep in thought and morose after we talked to the teacher."

"Just considering the sands of time," Tom replied which left Brad more confused than when he started.

"Let's try to get the university and Parkwood administrators done after lunch while the story is still somewhat contained."

They drove back to the station and split up to write up notes and eat before meeting again at 1:30 that afternoon to drive to the university.

The university campus is composed of Western University, and affiliates Brescia University, Huron University College, Kings University College and London Health Sciences Centre Hospital.

Tom and Brad entered through the campus entrance located at 1151 Richmond Street.

They drove to the administration office and were directed to Western's Ivey Business School located at 1255 Western Road and the office of the dean.

As they waited in the reception area for the dean, Brad read a printed history outline of the school.

In 1922, Ivey began in the basement of Western's University College, a small part of the Faculty of Arts program. Now Ivey takes its place on the global stage, standing as one of the world's leading business schools. Take a walk-through Ivey's history, from the basement of University College to the boardrooms of some of the top organizations in the world.

Dean Jones came out to the waiting area to greet them, and after shaking hands and introductions, Tom explained that they were here to ask some questions regarding Frank Shepherd's work at the Ivey School and any background that they can give them about his students, etc.

Tom noticed that the dean seemed reluctant to talk with them and had not invited them into his office.

"I don't know how I can help you. It's a tragedy what Frank and his wife are going through with the loss of their daughter."

"Can we go someplace more private and discuss?" Tom questioned.

"I guess I have a few moments to spare would you like to come into my office."

As they walked into his office, the dean asked if they would like a cup of coffee or water and Tom and Brad responded, "No thanks."

"We don't want to take up more of your time then necessary," Brad commented. Tom looked at Brad noting the slight tinge of sarcasm in his voice and realized that Brad had also picked up on the dean's reluctance to be interviewed.

After they had settled into the dean's office Tom asked, "Can you describe Frank Shepherd's work here at the school and his relationship to the staff and students?"

"Frank has been a professor here for some time and he has taught longer then I have been dean at this institution. As you are aware, we are an international institution with students from different parts of the globe studying here.

"I have been engaged in faculty social activities that Frank and his wife Elizabeth have attended but did not know them outside of the university."

"Can you tell us how Frank got along with the other staff and in particular any issues or concerns?"

"None that I am aware of, but this is a large faculty and we have a number of professors and staff. My role here is to oversee the operation and academic standards of the school and not to be involved in any petty politics or disputes between individuals."

"I understand that," Tom continued, "But you must be aware of any disputes, complaints filed by students regarding grades etc. Basically, any disgruntled faculty or students relating to Frank Shepherd."

"I am afraid I cannot help you as I am not aware of any information in that regards. I can have my assistant research the files and provide any documentation we might have but I doubt there will be anything. Frank is a good man and a good professor in line with the high standards we maintain at this institution."

"My colleague will give you his card, please have your assistant send along a report of what she discovers. Hopefully that will answer our questions and we will not need to return for a more extensive investigation into your internal files with our own people."

"That would be highly irregular," Dean Jones responded.

"Don't worry," Brad replied, "if we need to come back we will have a search warrant for your cooperation and our own people to dig into your files, so we do not tie up your time."

After they had left the office, Tom commented to Brad that the crack about the warrant and the dean's time was a might harsh since they had no real basis to delve into the files, as this was only background information.

"That guy burned my butt with his attitude and I wanted to let him sweat a little to bring him off his high horse."

The two detectives rode in silence as they traveled from the Ivey Business School over to Richmond Street and passed the downtown to the south of London to the Parkwood Rehabilitation Centre.

The London Parkwood Rehabilitation Institute was located at 550 Wellington Road South where Tom and Brad entered the main mental health care building. After identifying themselves as police, they asked reception to see the director of nursing regarding some questions they needed to ask.

Tom perused a history of Parkwood while he and Brad waited for the director of nursing.

Parkwood had been established in 1874 by the Women's Christian Association for 'the distribution of charity and the care of the poor and sick.' The building was renamed as Parkwood Hospital in 1894 The hospital operated as a 'home for incurables' at various locations in London moving to its current Westminster Campus site in 1985, built at a cost of $45 million. In 1989, the Western Counties Wing linked to Parkwood by the Arthur J Hobbins building was officially opened by Her Majesty Queen Elizabeth the Queen Mother.

Parkwood has grown to become one of the largest specialized chronic care hospitals in Ontario serving London, Southwestern Ontario, and Canadian Veterans.

A lady in a nurse's lab coat approached them and introduced herself as Susan Long, director of nursing staff at Parkwood and invited them to come with her to her office.

"Can you tell me what this is about?" she queried after they entered her office.

"We would like to ask you some questions regarding Elizabeth Shepherd, her duties here and any concerns that may have been raised regarding patients or their families?"

"Elizabeth is a good nurse and care giver. Hopefully this is not due to any patient related complaints."

"No," Tom replied. "This is part of the investigation resulting from the fire and death of her daughter earlier this week."

"O my goodness. I know Elizabeth has been off on bereavement for her daughter's death, but I was not aware it was connected to the story in the news media about the fire. The news reported the death as a homicide!"

"We are investigating the death as suspicious at this time and presumed to be a deliberate act. We just need to check out all possible concerns as part of our background investigation. How would you describe Elizabeth's work here at the hospital?"

"She is a wonderful person and nurse, caring and attentive to the patients in the rehabilitation ward where she works. The rehabilitation ward handles patients with traumatic injuries that are admitted for specialized rehabilitation services and care."

Brad asked, "Was there any disputes with fellow employees that you are aware of or with patients or their families who may have been disgruntled?"

"No, everyone worked well with Elizabeth and reports from patients and family have been extremely complimentary. Let me pull her file."

Ms. Long went on her computer and pulled up Elizabeth Shepherd's personal file.

"Everything in her file is complimentary, no disciplinary reports, and no noted issues or concerns. Elizabeth is a model employee and exceptional nurse."

"Thanks for your time," Tom stated. "We appreciate your cooperation as we investigate this tragedy."

"I feel terrible," Ms. Long responded. "Is it okay if we contact the Shepherds and send flowers during this time?"

"Not an issue as far as we are concerned," Brad replied. "We would appreciate you not discussing this interview with other staff or the press as we want to keep speculation to a minimum."

Tom and Brad left the Parkwood Institute, and Tom noted that at this point they had not found anything tangible regarding a possible motive for the homicide.

"Let's call it a night," Tom commented, "we should have the forensics and corners reports by late Thursday or Friday, and maybe they will give us a lead or something more tangible to go on."

It was Friday, the morning of the fifth day after the initial call out to the crime scene when the forensic report on the home break-in, arson and the autopsy landed on Tom's desk.

During the past four days, the news media had reported daily updates regarding the homicide and fire. The department media liaison had reminded the media that the investigation was early and that detectives were gathering information. A press conference was scheduled for this morning and the media liaison officer would be providing an official update and releasing the name of the victim. The briefing to prepare the media relations officer had occurred first thing when Tom and Brad had arrived. They considered the news that would be on the noon hour and evening broadcasts and agreed the liaison officer would have no real substantive information except the release of the name. They realized this would start the 'official' questions regarding what exactly the police were doing to solve this 'horrendous' crime. It would certainly provide fodder for politicians and community activists.

Tom sighed as he considered the 'new' era of police work and what everyone in the public assumed with the rash of police crime shows that had been on TV. The public now had an expectation that police could simply view a crime scene, collect samples, take them back to the lab, and within twenty-four hours have the case all neatly tied up. People did not understand that solving crimes took time and hard work to uncover the facts regarding motives and suspects.

In this age of instant gratification, the internet and television had become the arbitrary standard that people expected.

Tom chuckled to himself remembering a story his brother-in-law had told him. He worked as a nuclear lab technician at a major hospital. A lady had come in for testing, and when he had completed the scans, she asked him what was wrong with her. He told her that the results would be sent to her physician for review and the physician would get back to her. Her response was 'Dr. House' could tell what was wrong just by looking at her. He was slightly baffled and asked if Dr. House was her physician and she replied, "No, he is on the television, and he would know right away what's wrong." She had honestly equated the TV medical show doctor with the reality of medicine.

Get back to reality tommy boy, Tom reminded himself and settled at his desk with his fresh cup of coffee and the report.

Results of the arson investigation – the scene of the fire – was contained to the single bedroom located at the side of the house on the first floor.

A home water sprinkler system installed in the residence had engaged to extinguish the flames and limited the potential spread and fire damage from reaching the balance of the structure.

The report concluded that the fire had been intentionally set. The accelerant residue tested positive for mineral turpentine and verified the initial scene conclusion of the vice chief due to the odor and burn pattern on the floor, bed, wall, and curtains.

The following sketch indicates the lay out of the room, location of the fire, and the positioning of the victim.

Crime Scene Sketch:
Room size 3 meters x 3 meters
Window (closed and locked).

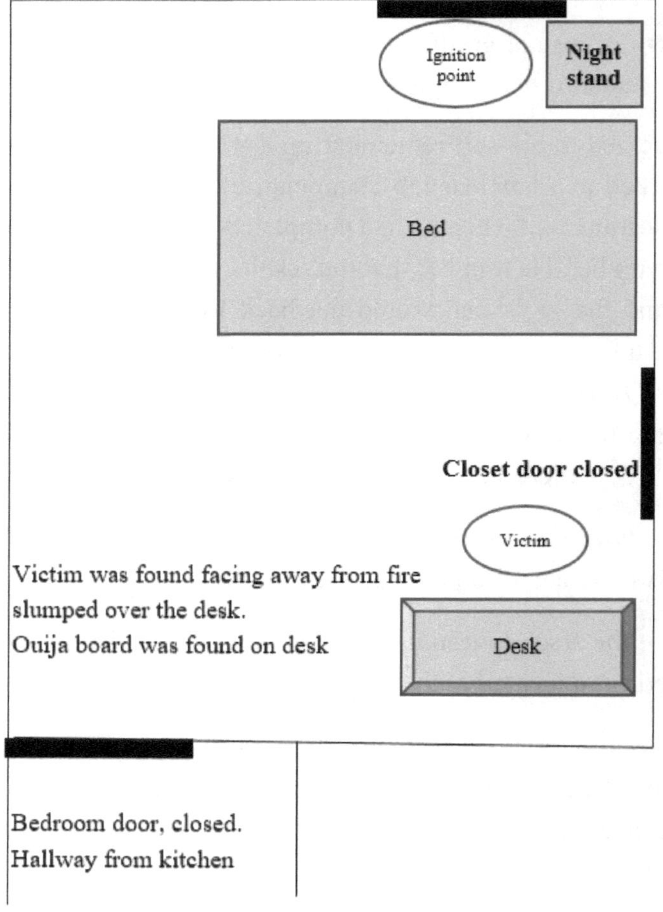

Autopsy Report:

Description of deceased: Victim was a female, Caucasian, age 16 and in relatively good health based on the information provided by the parents.

Conclusion: Victim had died from asphyxiation due to smoke inhalation.

The victim also sustained a non-lethal injury to the back of the skull resulting from blunt force trauma.

The wound was approximately 7.62 centimeters in length and consisted of a small curved indentation about 5 centimeters in depth. Weapon was likely a metal bar based on the metal slivers and blue paint chips found in the wound.

There were no drugs or foreign substances in the victim's blood stream.

The CID crime scene investigation report followed.

Investigator noted signs of forced entry into the kitchen through the back door. Scuff marks on the wooden frame beside the lock indicated the door had been pried open using some form of pry bar or similar object.

Nothing else appeared to have been disturbed in the house apart from the victim's bedroom.

The home owners returned to the scene with investigators on Thursday morning and verified that no articles had been removed from the premises including, jewelry, electronic equipment, and a small quantity of cash sitting on the nightstand in the master bedroom.

Nothing was noted as missing from the scene except for the diary of Deborah Shepherd which her mother stated was kept in her desk drawer in her bedroom. A search of the bedroom and personal belongings did not turn up the missing diary.

Deborah was known to keep daily entries in her diary, but her parents had not read it as they felt that would have been an invasion of her privacy.

A cell phone, iPad, and laptop computer belonging to Deborah was taken into evidence by the forensics identification unit for further analysis of online activity as part of the investigation.

Based on the investigation, forensics had concluded that the break in was a deliberate act, with the intent to murder Deborah Shepherd and cover the crime by setting the fire in the bedroom, by person or persons unknown at this point in time.

Access to the rear of the Shepherds' home appears to have likely come from the woodlot due to the identification of a muddy shoe print on the back step of the home. The woodlot runs along the back-lot lines of the houses on the East side of Jarvis Street.

A search was undertaken in the woodlot behind the Shepherds' home for any evidence of entry by that means.

Standing water was identified in the woodlot directly behind the Shepherds' property and mud puddles were evident throughout the woodlot.

The search of the woodlot did not turn up any usable evidence regarding the identification of the perpetrator(s).

On the desk in the victim's room was noted an Ouija board which was dusted for fingerprints and contained only the victim's prints. The victim's hands were in close proximity to the Ouija board.

Forensics collected photographs and fingerprints from the rear door, kitchen, hallway, and bedroom, but only family member's fingerprints were a match to evidence collected. It is concluded that the perpetrator(s) most likely wore gloves during the break in and homicide.

Tom paused from reading the reports to look up information regarding the Ouija board more out of curiosity then whether the fact that the Ouija board may relate to the incident.

*The **ouija** also known as a **spirit board** or **talking board**, is a flat board marked with the letters of the alphabet, the numbers 0–9, the words 'yes,' 'no,' 'hello' (occasionally), and 'goodbye,' along with various symbols and graphics. It uses a small heart-shaped piece of wood or plastic called a planchette. Participants place their fingers on the planchette, and it is moved about the board to spell out words. 'Ouija' is a trademark of Hasbro Inc. in the United States, but is often used generically to refer to any talking board. According to Hasbro, players take turns asking questions and then 'wait to see what the planchette spells out' for them.*

Following its commercial introduction by businessman Elijah Bond on July 1, 1890, the Ouija board was regarded as a parlor game unrelated to the occult until American spiritualist Pearl Curran popularized its use as a divining tool during World War 1. Spiritualists believed that the dead were able to contact the living and reportedly used a talking board very similar to a modern Ouija board at their camps in Ohio in 1886 to ostensibly enable faster communication with spirits.

Tom returned his attention to the report:

The unit had collected interview reports from the neighbors.

The first interview was with Elliott Carson as he lived directly beside the Shepherds and his back yard was separated by a wooden fence from the Shepherds' property and also connected to the woodlot at the back.

---

5 Wikipedia.org/Ouija

Mr. Carson stated that he was home at the time of the incident but would have been in the shower at the time it occurred. He indicated that he had not heard any unusual noise or observed any activity until the fire and emergency response vehicles arrived. He stated he looked out the window at the front of the house to observe the response vehicle activity.

He also commented on the fact that he did not know the Shepherds well as he had moved into his current home 10 months earlier and had only seen them in the yard or on the street. His contact was merely to acknowledge each other and say hello. Regarding the daughter, he has seen her on the street but was not familiar with her either. He did not observe much activity regarding other teenagers etc. coming over.

Mr. Carson is approximately 30 years old, black hair, full beard, 1.7 meters in height.

The second documented interview was with Joan and Allan Johnson, husband and wife who reside directly across the road from the Shepherds' house.

Joan is approximately 65 years of age, grey hair, 1.6 meters in height and Allan is approximately 67 years of age, 1.8 meters in height.

Mr. Johnson stated that they were retired, and both had been home at the time of the incident. They have no view of the Shepherds' back yard or the woodlot behind the Shepherds' home. They had been alerted to a problem by the sirens and arrival of the fire department and emergency vehicles.

They commented that they had gone out to the front yard to see what was happening around 7:15 or 7:20 but the fire department was simply cordoning off the home, so they assumed that either there had been a small fire or some other form of emergency.

When the police arrived and removed a body from the home, they were quite distressed, as they have been living across from the Shepherds for over 16 years since the Shepherds had moved into their home.

They confirmed that they knew Deborah Shepherd well as she has grown up on this street. They described her as a withdrawn child, and they did not see her with many other friends especially now that she was a teenager. They felt that Debbie was kind of a lonely child.

The parents were friendly, and they had talked over the years but had not been involved socially due to the age difference between them and the Shepherds.

Joan did mention that the Johnson's have a security system in their house with a camera that faces out onto the street.

Forensics verified that they have obtained a copy of the security footage during the time period leading up to the incident.

A review of the security footage did not provide any visual views of the woodlot and the back of the Shepherds' home but showed the front of the house. No activity was noted at the Shepherds until the arrival of the fire department and emergency response activity. The forensics report noted that the security footage showed the Johnsons and other neighbors in the front yards and across the street who came to watch during the emergency activity.

Nothing suspicious was noted and all those in attendance were either neighbors or media representatives who had arrived on the scene.

After reviewing the reports, Tom asked Brad to come into his office to take the reports to review separately. He also asked Brad to contact the family of the friend that had moved away, Mary Summers and arrange for them to meet with the family on Monday morning at their home in Simcoe.

"We will get together after lunch and compare notes after we both have had a chance to review the reports and see if anything strikes us."

Brad acknowledged the plan and took the reports and left to review them at his desk.

For the balance of the morning, Tom took the opportunity to work on the stack of paperwork on his desk and catch up on everything that had been happening over the past week.

Beside the high-profile investigation of the Shepherd fire and homicide, the routine of police life in London had continued. Tom and Brad had been called to assist in regard to the attempted sexual assault of a student on the Fanshawe College campus and an ongoing investigation of multiple vehicle thefts linked to gang activity that had occurred over the past several months.

Late July of this year, Statistics Canada had released its latest data on the crime severity index across Canada, and London's was up by three percent from 2016 figures.

The report pointed to four causes for the rise including motor vehicle theft, sexual assault, breaking and entering, and theft of $5000 or under. The rise was offset by a decrease in homicides between 2016 and 2017.

A Canadian Broadcasting Company (CBC) report on the rise in London crime rate had quoted London Deputy Chief Steve Williams: 'You have to have a closer look at the statistics to understand what that means. It doesn't necessarily mean it's more dangerous or anything like that. What complicates the numbers is that crimes are weighted. So, one less homicide in a year would have a much greater impact on the crime severity than one less break and enter.

As well if police launch a task force to crack down on an issue such as guns and gangs, the proactive work may result in a higher number of arrests and reported crimes involving weapons. That too could influence the crime severity rate.'

After lunch Tom and Brad reconvened in Tom's office to discuss the reports.

"One thing I want to do is to interview the student mentioned by Mr. Saunders, Nancy Graves. In addition, there may be some others we want to talk with after we interview the friend of Debbie Shepherd, Mary Summers."

Brad mentioned that forensics had the laptop, iPad, and cell phone that belonged to Debbie and that may help them understand what was going on in her life. Forensics noted there was some water damage from the sprinklers but nothing serious to prevent obtaining information off the electronic devices.

"Good point," Tom mused, "let's request forensics to give us a report as soon as possible on what was found and then we may want to take a closer look at anyone who pops up in that search.

"Well that's about all we can do on the Shepherd's case for today until we meet with the other contacts next week. Have a good weekend and we will get a fresh start Monday morning."

Tom spent the balance of the afternoon finalizing the paperwork he had started in the morning and considering any other items that had landed on his desk during the week while he had been engaged with the Shepherd's initial investigation.

It was 8:30 on Saturday morning when Tom finally rolled out of bed. Ann simply curled up tighter under the covers and commented on the fact that in another seven weeks this would be his daily routine since he would not need to get up and get ready to go into the office.

Tom simply grunted as he headed to the washroom.

"I'll get breakfast ready," Ann said, "and then we are going for a drive over to Sparta and visit the shops for the day."

"Is there a reason that we are road tripping?" Tom queried.

"I don't want you spending your Saturday sitting here and thinking about work and cases. It's time you start to adjust to a different lifestyle to get ready for the big day."

"You make it sound like I am suddenly going to be old and useless with nothing to do just because I will not be going to the police station."

"Not old and useless just different," Ann went off to the kitchen to put on the coffee and start cooking breakfast.

Oh, my goodness, Tom thought, *what have I done by filling out those retirement papers. It's time I looked into other hobbies and activities to fill my time. I wonder if Ann truly realizes that my retirement will affect her as well, and she may not find it so enjoyable for her, me being underfoot.*

Ann had been a stay-at-home mom while the boys grew up and had developed a standard routine of activities she participated in as an empty nester. She obviously liked her independence, and Tom wondered how this change in daily life would affect their overall relationship.

He looked deeply into his face in the mirror as he prepared to shave noting again his grey receding hairline.

"I don't look that old," Tom commented out loud to himself, "but I am beginning to feel old." Tom knew that it was all in his mind as he prepared for the inevitable adjustment that retirement would bring.

After breakfast, the two of them headed out for the one-hour drive to Sparta. Tom took the back roads and stayed off the busy 401 Highway, so they could observe the fields and the greenery as they drove on the two-lane road leaving London on Richmond Street till they connected with provincial highway #3 just outside St. Thomas. The leaves on the trees were still green but the fall would be here soon when the fall colors would turn the trees foliage from green to brilliant red, gold, and yellow.

Tom entered Sparta, a quaint historic village that was founded by a group of Pennsylvania Quakers who settled here in 1822. Many of the descendants of those early settlers still live in the area. The 'downtown' consisted of the crossroad intersection of two roads that ran through the town. The buildings, business fronts, and stores remain preserved in the same original style. Ann loved the history and reading the historical information plaques on the storefronts that described the building and its evolution of uses over the years.

On the left-hand side of Quaker Road, just north of the village is the Quaker Meeting House that is still in use to this day.

Other business consisted of the Sparta Country Candles 'general store,' art studios, museums, and the Sparta Tea House.

---

6 www.spartaquakers.com
7 www.spartacandles.com

As a natural component of their visit to Sparta, Tom and Ann went into the Sparta Tea House to relax over a cup of tea and homemade confectionaries.

Looking around the tearoom, Tom observed the hundreds of teapots collected by the owners over the years. Large and small, decorative and whimsical from around the world.

The teahouse had been featured on the TV show *Rescue Mediums* – The Sparta Tea House episode – when investigators came to see what they could find about the 'haunted tearoom in Sparta.'*

---

8 www.spartahouse.com
* Rescue Mediums, Season 4, Episode #42.

After spending time wandering about the stores and buildings and having lunch, they drove the short distance outside Sparta to the Steed & Co. Lavender Farm.

This was one place that Tom really enjoyed visiting a couple of times during the summer to simply walk the pathways amongst the lavender rows and listen to the ever-present humming of the masses of bees that were gathering nectar in the flowers. The sound and the smell were somehow relaxing and refreshing in a way that Tom found hard to describe.

It was time to head back to London. Ann wanted to stop into the Farmer's and Artisan's Market that was held every Saturday at the London Western District Fairground on King Street.

They spent the remainder of the afternoon strolling through the market, selecting fresh fruits and vegetables as well as some pastries to enjoy throughout the coming week.

"That was nice," Ann commented as they arrived at home, "It's good for us to get out together and connect more."

"You may find yourself getting fed up with 'connecting' with me in a few months," Tom mused.

9 www.spartahouse.com

Sunday morning was a long-established routine for the couple.

They were lifelong members of 'Woodfield Community of Christ' congregation in London.

The church got its name from its location in the historic Woodfield district, downtown London.

The congregation had its roots in London, having been in existence for over 140 years with the establishment of its first church building in 1875.

In 1916, the congregation had built a red brick church on Maitland Street in London. In 1997, the congregation broke ground on a new church home at 615 Colborne Street which was to become the Woodfield Community of Christ.

Tom and Ann had attended the Maitland Street Church, and Tom had been involved as a member of the building committee in the task to designing and overseeing the building of the new church home.

The change in location had occurred because the Thames Valley District School Board needed to purchase the original church property on Maitland Street as part of a project to build a new school sports field in London. The school board had traded the congregation the property on Maitland Street with the property on Colborne Street that was owned by the school board. The school district also paid to purchase and tear down the existing church.

Since the original 1916 church was being demolished, the school authority had allowed the congregation to take the original pews, and the historically significant stained-glass windows from the old building to install in the new church.

Tom loved the peace and calmness of the sanctuary where he could sit and contemplate the stained glass windows.

The stained glass window on the side of the sanctuary was titled 'The Good Shepherd' and depicted Christ as the Shepherd, the main window behind the pulpit was dated 1919 and had been moved from the congregation's original church on Maitland Street when the new church had been built.

He remembered their sons growing up in this church home, the youth activities, volleyball games in the gymnasium, and movie nights in the church

---

10 Woodfield Community of Christ, 615 Colborne street, London
11 Woodfield Community of Christ, 615 Colborne street, London

library. Arranging transportation so they could attend youth church camps and teen gatherings.

Tom felt a wave of remorse and sadness for the Shepherds.

The body of Debbie had been released Friday to the family, and they were now back in their 'home' preparing to bury their child.

Tom realized that as part of his job he needed to remain distant and disconnected from the victims and the families of those who are involved in his investigations and up to now he was successful at doing that. Maybe it was the impending change in his own life that was making him feel so much for the loss of Frank and Elizabeth.

The thought of burying your own child and not watching them grow, have relationships, marry, and have children of their own felt like a tragedy too hard to bear.

Tom and Ann had two sons.

Kevin the youngest who was in his final year at the University at Western Ontario studying engineering.

Their older son Tom Jr. was married and had two children of his own. They lived in Guelph, a city that was a ninety-minute drive from London. Tom Jr. worked at the University of Guelph Research Innovation office.

Tom Jr. had shared the Innovation office mandate with his father when he accepted the position which meant the move to Guelph:

The Research Innovation Office helps transform the University of Guelph's world-class research into innovations that change lives and improve life. We connect research to the world and use on-campus innovation to foster positive changes for the community, government, and industry.

Technology Transfer staff work with faculty, staff, and students to protect their intellectual property and maximize its potential economic, social, and environmental benefits.

Industry Liaison links companies with research and development needs to University of Guelph expertise and resources to form valuable research partnerships and leverage funding opportunities.

New Venture Creation is the hub for business incubation and acceleration at the University of Guelph, providing resources and knowledge to help entrepreneurs get their product to market faster and grow successfully.

Knowledge Mobilization promotes a two-way flow of information between researchers and the community, government and industry, ensuring that research is positioned to inform decisions and increase impact.

The Research Innovation Office is where U of G ingenuity meets the marketplace, and great ideas reach their full potential.

Tom often marveled at how his two sons had chosen their fields of study and ultimate careers. He usually commented that they had inherited their brains from their mother and their audacity from him. But he often considered internally the fact that neither of his sons had shown any desire to follow in their father's footsteps with police work.

After church, the family would gather in the afternoon at the grant family home for a family supper. It was a tradition and time of the week Tom looked forward to when he could simply concentrate on his grandchildren and listen to the family chatter.

Chapter 2:
Week Seven

Monday morning September 17th started much like every other week with the exception that Tom was now seven weeks from his retirement date.

He would need to make another appointment with the personnel department in the next couple of weeks to arrange for his exit interview on his final day of active duty when he would turn in his identification, gun, keys, and become a 'regular' citizen.

Upon arrival at the office, he contacted Brad and made sure everything was arranged for the trip to Simcoe to meet with Mary Summers and her parents to interview her about Deborah.

"We are set to meet Mary's parents in front of the Simcoe Composite School at 11:00 a.m., and then we will have the school arrange for us to meet with Mary during her lunch break period. It will take us approximately an hour and a half to drive there so we need to leave by 9 or shortly thereafter," Brad remarked.

"Fine. Come to my office just before nine this morning and we will head out."

Tom settled at his desk with his cup of morning coffee to spend the hour preparing his thoughts.

At 8:50 Brad came to Tom's office, and they headed out for the drive to Simcoe. As they approached the town of Simcoe on Highway #3, Tom observed the fields and crops. Sporadically, he noted individual fields of tobacco plants which brought back memories from his youth.

He had grown up in Simcoe and when he was a teenager, tobacco growing was the number one cash crop in the area. The work in the fields started in spring with planting, hoeing, and as the plants grew to a height of around six feet he would be hired to 'top and sucker' the plants. This entailed walking down the rows and breaking off the flower tops and picking out the small leaves that would sprout between the stalk and the larger leaves so that the plant put all its energy into the growing of the main leaves.

He had spent his summers working in the fields, and in mid-august through the first frost of late September he worked picking the leaves or 'priming' as it was called. The money was good as the primers would get paid by the kiln which was the small curing buildings that the tobacco would be hung in and heated to dry before they would be sent to the Tobacco Auction house in Delhi. Over the course of the day, you would prime enough tobacco leaves to fill one or one and a half kilns. This represented a high wage in the 1960s, especially for a teenager.

Tom had been 15 when he had spent his first harvest season as a 'primer' and that year they still used a horse drawn tobacco 'boat' to haul in the harvested leaves. The priming crew consisted of six primers who each would walk down between the rows of tobacco picking off the bottom three leaves on the row beside him as the plants leaves ripened. The leaves turned a yellow color when they were ready to pick starting with the 'sand leaves' as the first picking and then going back for each level referred to as the firsts, seconds, etc. until you cleaned off the smaller top leaves called the 'tips.'

The newest member generally got the boat row as the horse would follow behind this person which resulted in you spending the day being butted by the horse as you walked along bent over to the level of the leaves you were picking. Tom's back tightened with an unconscious sympathetic ache as he reminisced about the work.

He recalled watching the National Film Board of Canada documentary *The Back-Breaking Leaf* by Terence Macartney Filgate,[12] which portrayed the tobacco harvest in the 1950s. The work was much bleaker then as compared to the farms where he worked just ten years later. Being local, he worked on the same farm every summer and the crew were mostly his friends and had shared a spirit of comradery.

The work was hard, and in the early morning when dew covered the fields you would get soaking wet from the plants, then by the afternoon you would be sweating in the sun's heat. In the fall with the final picking of the top leaves, the work would be cold and miserable but the tobacco crop provided a good source of summer income for local and migrant farm workers.

That all had now ended as the auction houses had closed and the tobacco companies moved to contracting smaller crops to meet declining demand until only a few tobacco farms remained.

The rest had changed to cash crops, ginseng, and peanuts as alternatives so that the summer tobacco employment work had disappeared for the local and migrant workers to a significant degree.

They arrived at the Wilson Avenue front entrance to Simcoe Composite School at 10:45.

Tom looked at the school's front entrance and remembered his high school years attending this institution. The front had not changed since he attended, and he reminisced about his time walking the halls, attending classes, and eating in the cafeteria. He remembered the gymnasium and the school music

---

12 https://blog.nfb.ca/blog/2016/08/19/photo-friday-back-breaking-leaf/

room tucked in behind the front of the gymnasium where he had spent one semester trying to learn to play the violin in music class.

Possibly the violin was something he could take up again after he retired.

At the front door of the school, a couple was standing so Tom and Brad approached them to see if they were the Summers.

"Good morning," Brad commented, "Are you Robert and Alice Summers?"

"Yes, we are," they replied.

"My name is Detective Tom Grant, and this is Detective Brad Logan from the London Police Department," Tom stated showing his credentials and shaking their hands.

"We will not keep you long we just need to ask Mary some questions regarding her former friend, Deborah Shepherd in London."

"We read about the terrible incident at the Shepherd's home, Frank and Elizabeth must be devastated. How could this have happened?"

"We are still in the early stages of the investigation and looking for any leads or information that can provide us any assistance at this time."

The four of them entered the front door of the school and proceeded to the school administration office.

The school administrative secretary was aware of their expected arrival and she had arranged for Mary to come to the principal's office when her class broke for lunch period at 11.

When Mary arrived, Tom noted that she was a young lady about the same age as Debbie with black hair. She was non-descript in appearance and did not stand out amongst the other teenagers. It was obvious why she and Debbie had become friends as they shared the same average appearance and introverted nature.

"Hi Mary," Tom started, "I am Tom Grant, and this is Brad Logan. We are investigating the death of your friend Debbie Shepherd in London and wanted to ask you some background questions regarding Debbie and the other students in London. This will not take long and we will try to be considerate as I know you are upset about Debbie."

Mary sat looking down at the desk between them with her hands clutched in her lap and seemed reluctant to make eye contact.

"What can you tell us about Debbie?"

"Debbie was my friend. We hung out together at school and on weekends. Neither of us had a lot of other friends. Debbie was close to her grandmother and it hurt her when she past."

"Did Debbie have any problems at school say with other students?"

"There was one girl in our class, Nancy Graves. She was one of the popular girls, and she was always picking on us. She and her friends would put up drawings of Debbie and me with nasty comments on bulletin boards, and she was relentless in teasing Debbie online calling her terrible names and making up stories about her."

"We talked to the principal," Ann Summers broke in, "Told them about what the other students were doing to Debbie and our daughter, but the school did nothing about it. They said it was simply teenagers being teenagers, and since the other students had not physically done anything against the girls we needed to just let it pass. They said that eventually the other kids would grow tired of doing it and quit if we were just patient."

"I was not willing to let Mary be harassed like that," her father stated. "So, we moved last summer to Simcoe and transferred Mary to this school. The principal here has a no tolerance policy for any type of bullying."

"Nancy has stopped posting all the mean things about me," Mary stated, "but I know they have still been saying nasty things about Debbie."

"Can you give us the names of the other students?" asked Brad.

"The main ones were Sarah Hendricks and Jason Bradley. They were in the same homeroom as we were last year. I still have some of the things they posted on my cell phone."

"Would you mind showing us?" Tom remarked.

Mary brought up some emails that had been sent to her and Debbie last year on her screen.

One was a picture of her and Debbie that had been photoshopped so that they looked like they were kissing, and the caption was 'Fag Friends get it on!' The second one was a picture of the two of the girls with a bull's eye on their faces and stated 'The target is in sight. Ready, Aim, Fire!'

Tom asked Mary if she could forward those to his email and thanked her very much for the information.

"You are a brave young lady and should never have had to be subjected to this garbage."

"We will find out who took your friend's life, and we will have a strong discussion with the school principal about his actions regarding the bullying."

Tom and Brad thanked Mary and her parents for their help and left the school.

After stopping for lunch, they headed back to London and spent the afternoon going over the report from the department's information technology technician regarding the search through Debbie's laptop, iPad, and iPhone. They reviewed entries that were retrieved from the emails and web posting of Nancy Graves, Sarah Hendricks, and Jason Bradley regarding Deborah Shepherd.

The entries were generally mean and petty bordering on harassment but did not appear to rise to the level of a hate crime. They were stupid and uncaring in nature, and Tom looked forward to having a stern and candid discussion with these three teenagers and their parents.

They paused when they got to one posting which was of particular interest on Jason's page.

It was a picture of Debbie with flames encircling her face and the caption read 'I am the God of Hell Fire, and I bring your fire.'

In the background, the Arthur Brown song *Fire* was playing. [13]

Brad searched the lyrics for the song on the internet:

The wording of the song proclaimed that the listener was going to burn which left both Brad and Tom concerned due to the circumstances of Debbie's death.

...[14]

"Brad, I believe we need to have a long chat with this Jason. Let's contact the parents and bring in these three for a discussion tomorrow morning. Then I want to go and have a heart to heart with the principal again."

"Will do," Brad replied and left Tom's office.

Tom was both disgusted and discouraged by reading the comments and pictures these teens had posted in such a spiteful manner against the two girls and could not understand how this could happen. What would affect these youth to be so hurtful? Maybe the experts were right regarding the mentality where doing things in cyber space left people with a sense that what they were doing was not in some way 'real.' A form of electronic anonymity that took away individual good sense and reason.

In this era of electronic texting and messaging, it was eerie how true those words had become.

---

13 *Fire* is a 1968 song written by Arthur Brown, Vincent Crane, Mike Finesilver and Peter Ker.
14 *Fire* is a 1968 song written by Arthur Brown, Vincent Crane, Mike Finesilver and Peter Ker.

At home that evening, Tom read in the newspaper that the funeral of Debbie Shepherd was scheduled for Wednesday afternoon at 2:00 p.m., and the burial would follow at the Woodlands Cemetery on Springbank Road after the service.

He made a note in his calendar to attend the funeral.

Tuesday at 9:00 a.m., Brad had contacted the families of the three youths they wished to interview along with their parents and they were all waiting in the interview rooms.

"Let's start with Nancy as she appeared to be the ring leader of this little band," Tom remarked.

They walked into the interview room where a pretty blonde teenager sat between two adults, presumably her parents.

She had a sullen and defiant look on her face, and Tom could see that she was not going to be very cooperative. Tom's first impression was that she was one who had been overindulged and spoiled.

Settle down, tommy boy, don't let your own feelings pre-judge, Tom thought to himself.

After the detectives identified themselves and were introduced to Mary's parents, John and Hazel Graves, Tom stated, "We are here this morning to interview Nancy regarding her interactions with Deborah Shepherd."

John Graves cut in stating, "I am a lawyer as well as Nancy's father and I have no intention of letting you harass my daughter in any form. Keep your questions directed at me, and I will advise if she will answer."

"Mr. Graves, this is a homicide investigation in which your daughter has become a person of interest due to information we have received regarding actions that she has engaged in towards Deborah Shepherd."

"My daughter has not associated with the Shepherd girl, and they are not friends, so I find the fact that you have brought us here to be highly irregular and quite frankly a waste of taxpayer resources."

"Mr. Graves, you have the right to ask questions at the appropriate time during this interview, but I warn you if you continue to hamper the interview we will seek action against you for impeding our investigation."

John Graves sat back in his chair and crossed his arms demonstrating that he, like his daughter, had no intention of cooperating.

"Susan, what was your relationship with Deborah Shepherd?" Tom asked.

"She was in my home room class, but I did not really know her. She was not the type to be part of the crowd I hang around with. She was funny looking and frankly kind of dull."

"Did you engage in actions that were designed to belittle and make fun of Debbie both in school and online?"

Mr. Graves broke in again, "I am not sure what you have heard or what someone has said about my daughter Detective Grant but I assure you she has never been involved in anything derogatory against this other girl. And I am not going to allow you to harass her."

"If you wish to talk about harassment," Brad intervened, "let's take a look at these online postings and comments that your daughter has authored towards Debbie Shepherd."

Brad opened a manila folder and laid out screen print copies of the emails and postings that Nancy had put online on the table in front of Nancy and her parents.

"We also have testimony that Nancy and some of her friends posted derogatory material on bulletin boards in the school regarding Deborah and other students. These have been verified by our information technology department as being posted by Nancy amongst others and can be proven in court if necessary."

"As a lawyer Mr. Graves, I am sure you are aware of the federal and provincial laws regarding cyber bullying. Harassment is a crime under the Criminal Code defined as 'something a person does or says that makes someone fear for his or her safety or for the safety of others.' Even if the perpetrator does not intend to frighten someone, she or he can be charged with harassment if the target feels threatened."

"Another girl that has been the subject of your daughter's harassment so concerned her parents that they moved away from London in order to take their daughter away from the bullying and will testify to that fact."

"I am sure my daughter was only joking around and had no intention of harming the other girls," Nancy's mother broke in.

"I would like Nancy to answer our questions and speak for herself," Tom responded.

"We were just kidding around, we never touched Debbie or anyone else. I assume Mary Summers is the other person if that is what you want me to tell you. It was just for a laugh," Nancy now had a perceivable frightened tone in her voice. "We didn't mean any real harm it was all just fun."

John Graves now displayed a much more conciliatory nature when he leaned forward and made the statement, "I apologize for any childish actions my daughter may have committed. I can assure you we will take steps to ensure she learns from her mistake and will not do anything like this in the future."

"Nancy last Monday between 6 and 7:30 in the morning can you provide us with what you were doing and where you were during that time frame," Brad asked.

"I was home getting ready for school until the bus picked me up at 7:00, and then I was on the bus till we arrived at school."

"I was also home and can verify that Nancy was in our house until she caught the bus in front of our home," Mrs. Graves added.

Tom advised them that they were now free to go but that any further complaints regarding online harassment and bullying would be taken very seriously. As he looked at John Graves, he stated, "Counsellor I know I do not need to tell you that we will expend whatever resources we require to ensure that your daughter will be held accountable for any future actions, and if the family of the other girl in this investigation so chooses we will recommend that the crown attorney pursue legal action for harassment."

John Graves did not respond and the family were escorted from the interview room.

The family of Sarah Hendricks were brought into the interview room.

Tom and Brad went through the same discussion as they had with the Graves family.

The main difference was that the parents of Sarah were totally cooperative and afraid for their young daughter. Sarah broke down crying when she was questioned about the bullying and stated that it had been Nancy's idea.

They were just having fun but she didn't think that they were causing any harm.

She swore through her tears she would never do anything like that again and her parents shared that they were shocked by what had happened. They promised that they would ensure Sarah did not spend time with the Graves girl anymore and that Sarah was restricted from her cell phone and internet till they were sure she understood how wrong she had been.

Sarah shared that she too had been at home and then at school on the Monday morning during the time period in question. Her mother had driven her to the school just after 7:00 a.m. on her way to her work.

The Hendricks kept stating that they had raised their daughter better than this as the family left.

Brad shared that there was at least one teenage girl who was going to regret her choices. He was more skeptical about Nancy Graves.

The final interview was with Jason Bradley and his parents which went much like Sarah's except when Jason was asked regarding the online post he had made about Debbie and the reference to fire.

"I didn't intend anything by it. It was all part of making fun of Debbie. I was listening to the song on my computer when I got the idea to use it to refer to Debbie. It was just for a laugh. I did it weeks ago during summer vacation."

Tom commented on the fact that this was highly suspicious based on the fact that Debbie Shepherd's cause of death resulted from a fire that had been deliberately set in her home.

"I am really sorry," Jason said. "It was just to show Nancy and Sarah that I could come up with great posts about Debbie the same as they could. I didn't mean for anything like this to happen."

Jason's parents asked if they needed a lawyer and Brad told them the same as he had told Nancy's and Sarah's parents regarding the criminal and civil legality that could be associated with the youth's actions. He stated it would be up to the crown attorney and the parents of the girls to decide if they wished to proceed with any further legal action regarding the bullying and harassment.

With the interviews done, Tom and Brad spent the balance of the day going over the evidence, but up to this point in the investigation, nothing tangible regarding a viable motive or suspect was standing out.

On Wednesday, Tom decided to stop into the office of the high school principal at Debbie's school and have a chat about his lack of action regarding the bullying reports.

He laid out the online posts and actions of the students regarding harassing and bullying in the school on the principal's desk. Tom advised him that they had discussed this issue with the parents of Mary Summers and were aware they had logged bullying complaints with the principal.

Tom indicated his intention to send his report to the superintendent of schools regarding the principal's lack of action and would also provide it to the parents should they choose to take legal action for ignoring the complaints.

The principal was apologizing continuously stating he did not realize the extent of the students' actions. Tom was pleased to note that the principal was sweating visibly when he exited his office.

Good, Tom thought, *maybe that will give him something to think about for the rest of the day and he will take things more seriously regarding his duty to keep the kids safe in his school.* Tom had no sympathy for a person in a position of authority who did not follow through on his responsibility of care for those in his charge.

After lunch, Tom prepared to attend the funeral service for Debbie Shepherd. The funeral home was packed with friends and relatives who had come to grieve with Frank and Elizabeth.

Tom quietly surveyed the room. He saw individuals he had met from the university and hospital attending along with the neighbors from across the street. He recognized the Johnson's from the surveillance tape they had provided the police. He had noticed them standing with a small group in front of the crime scene tape after the emergency vehicles had responded.

Looking at those gathered at the funeral, he wondered which one on the tape had been the neighbor from next door, Elliot Carson.

He thought back to the reports and remembered that Elliot Carson had been in his early thirties, but he could not remember a man about that age among those on the surveillance tape.

No big deal, he thought, *just a point of curiosity.*

The funeral service lasted nearly 45 minutes before the coffin was carried by the pallbearers to the Funeral Hearst. The family and friends departed behind the Hearst in their vehicles for the internment at Woodlands Cemetery.

It was ironic in a way that Debbie would be buried in the cemetery on Springbank Drive, just a few blocks from her home.

At the station, Brad had put out a hotline public request asking for anyone who had seen anything suspicious around the time of the Shepherd's fire either on Jarvis Street or on Springbank Drive where the woodlot bordered the street.

Tom headed back to the station and spent the balance of the week working on other cases hoping for some breakthrough that could be investigated from the hotline. Brad kept him appraised of the fact that nothing substantial was coming in.

It was Friday afternoon and Ron Ralston had finished his lunch. He stood looking out of his seventh story apartment balcony located at Springbank on the Park on Springbank Drive. It was a beautiful day, and he was going for a run in Springbank Park on the pedestrian pathways.

The trees were just starting to show a hint of color change on the leaves, and he loved this time of the year and the parkland. Springbank Park was the reason he had moved to this apartment building that overlooked the canopy of trees.

The park was composed of 140 hectares (300 acres) that ran along a stretch of the Thames River and contained 30 kilometers of trails. It is also home to the children's attraction, Storybook Gardens, a family centered fun park with story tale themed activities and rides run by the City of London Parks Department since 1958.

Ron left the apartment building and crossed the street at the nearby corner where he entered into Springbank Park and proceeded on the walking path down into the park past the entrance to Storybook Gardens. This provided access to the paved walkway that he used as his jogging route that ran beside the river.

It was quiet with only the sounds of the birds and his foot beats as he ran along. He came to a spot where the paved pathway intersected with a dirt path so he left the pavement and proceeded along the dirt path. The route was covered by an overhead canopy formed from the branches of the large mature trees.

At one-point, Ron stopped to do calisthenics to stretch his legs against the trunk of an old oak tree. As he leaned against the tree bark, he glanced up and noticed the corner of a small book tucked inside a hollow in the tree above his head.

Curious, he reached up and pulled out the small white book. It was a diary. Ron decided to open it and see whom it belonged to. *Maybe someone is hiding this here so no one else can read it,* he chuckled to himself.

He opened the book to the front page where the name of the owner and author was transcribed.

'Property of Debbie Shepherd'

Ron immediately remembered the news stories last week about the Shepherd family that lived up the road on Jarvis Street off Springbank Drive.

The daughter had been identified in the press as Deborah Shepherd.

Ron carefully returned the book to where he had found it and took out his cell phone to dial the police.

CHAPTER THREE:
WEEK SIX

When Tom arrived at the station, he followed his normal routine of filling his cup with his morning coffee and went to his office. He glanced at his desk calendar and realized it was the last full week of September.

The message light on his desk phone was blinking steadily. Tom settled back into his chair and picked up the handset, entered his voice mail code and waited.

"Hi Tom, this is Pete, we got a call out Friday afternoon for forensics to attend a scene in Springbank Park. A passing jogger had located Debbie Shepherd's diary tucked into a tree hollow in the park. Give me a call and we can discuss."

Tom called Brad and told him to come to his office, when he arrived they called Pete in forensics.

"Hi Pete, this is Tom and Brad what have you got for us?"

"Ron Ralston, who lives on the seven-floor of an apartment building on Springbank Drive across from Springbank Park called in the fact that he had found the Shepherd girl's diary in a tree hollow while jogging on the walking trail in the park. Mr. Ralston waited at the scene till the officer arrived and he gave his statement to the attending officer. It appears Mr. Ralston was taking a routine jog and stopped to stretch against a tree where he noticed the book in a hollow just above eye level. He opened it, saw the name, and returned it to the tree hollow before calling police.

"The diary is definitely Debbie Shepherd's and we dusted for prints but only came up with Mr. Ralston's on the cover and Debbie's inside. There was one unidentified print on the page corner of the entry page for the Friday before the incident at the Shepherds' home, but it was badly smudged and did not come up with any matches in the criminal database.

"If I had a more specific individual's print for comparison we may be able to get a partial match but that's the best we have at this time."

"Thanks Pete, can you send over the diary when you are done processing it as I would like to go through it. Also, please send me the full address for the jogger so we can follow up with a more detailed interview."

Momentarily, Tom's cell phone text beeped with the address and phone number for Ron Ralston.

"What do you think?" queried Brad.

"We have not had anything solid from the hotline responses to this point, so this is likely our best lead if we can find anything substantive from the notes in the diary. Not holding my breath since the diary was the only thing taken, the perpetrator will have already gone through it to see if there was anything incriminating."

Brad dialed Ron Ralston's number listed on the contact information.

When Mr. Ralston answered, Brad introduced himself and asked if he would mind if the detectives came over for a follow up interview. Ron replied that he was free any time and they were welcome to come over to his apartment.

"We can be there within a half hour if that is suitable."

Ron agreed and advised the detectives to simply buzz his apartment number when they arrived, so he could let them in the front lobby.

They drove 15 minutes from the police station along Springbank Drive past the turn off on Jarvis Street that lead to the Shepherds' home.

Springbank on the Park was a luxury 12 story apartment building just before the intersection of Springbank Drive and Commissioners Road.

They entered the secure glassed circular front entrance and contacted Mr. Ralston on the intercom resulting in them being beeped into the building.

The lobby of the building was equipped with a fireplace, comfortable chairs and a glassed water wall where air bubbles rose from the floor to ceiling, highlighted by rotating different colored lighting.

"Interesting," Brad commented, "this place probably has a pool and all the amenities."

They rode the elevator up to the seventh floor which oddly was listed as the fifth floor on the elevator keypad. The first two floors which were the main entrance and lobby facing the front of the building were built into the side of the hill at the back. This resulted in the rear section of the first two floors being designated as the underground parking garage. The Ralston apartment was listed as the fifth floor but in reality, was seven floors up from the street on the front side of the building.

Ron Ralston met them at the apartment door. Tom and Brad introduced themselves and showed their identification.

"Hello Mr. Ralston, this should not take long we just need to verify the information that was taken Friday afternoon by the attending officer."

"No problem," Ron replied.

Ron was a gentleman in his late sixties, slender build and was in good health.

"Can you go through your actions on Friday afternoon?"

"I had finished my lunch and told my wife, Bridgett, I was going for a jog in the park which I do three or four times a week. We moved into this apartment building seven months ago when I retired. Bridgett and I moved to London to be closer to our family and grandkids."

Brad glanced out of the balcony doors overlooking the green blanket of trees and lush vegetation of Springbank Park. The view was spectacular emerging out of the tree canopy. You could see the top of the downtown high-rise buildings and the multi-story apartment complexes towards the north of London. He could really appreciate why the city of London was nicknamed the 'forest city' with this view.

"I went to the corner of Commissioners and crossed over to enter the park going down the pathway that leads past the entrance of Storybook Gardens. I turned right and jogged along the asphalt walking and biking track till I reached the point where the dirt-walking path intersects the asphalt. I like to run along the dirt path because its quiet and the tree cover provides shade against the sun.

"I started to get a small cramp in my leg, so I stopped at a large oak tree to stretch and do calisthenics to ease the cramps. As I was leaning against the tree trunk, I happened to look up and saw the corner of something sticking out of the hollow in the tree where a large limb grew out of the trunk. I reached up and retrieved a small book. When I opened it and saw Deborah Shepherd's name on the front inside cover, I immediately closed it and put it back as close as I could to how I found it, called the police and waited for them to arrive."

"Did you happen to see anyone in the area when you arrived or at any point in the past two weeks when you were out jogging?" Brad asked.

"Sorry but I don't pay much attention to other walkers and joggers but there are generally a number of different individuals using the trails when I go for my run."

"I want to thank you for your time," Brad commented, "If you happen to recall anything else that may seem unusual or significant, please give us a call."

Tom interjected, "One quick personal question. I was wondering how you are finding retirement?"

"First few months were an adjustment for me and my wife, establishing new routines and reaching an understanding of how each of us were reacting to the other being around all the time. In my working career, I traveled a fair deal and my wife got used to having periods of time when she was on her own, able to come and go as she wished without me being underfoot.

"Being home all the time we quickly realized that both of us needed time on our own, I have my den which allows me to spend time alone on my computer and write while she has her own space and can engage in endeavors that suit her."

"Appreciate the insight," Tom replied, "I will be retiring in a few weeks and was just curious."

The conversation had simply reaffirmed Tom's growing questions about his impending retirement and left him wondering again if he was making the right decision.

When they returned to the station, forensics had delivered the diary to Tom's desk along with Debbie's laptop, iPad, and cell phone.

They decided to start with the electronic equipment and began to scroll through the list of calls and texts that were on her phone.

There were not a lot of text conversations except between Debbie and her friend Mary. The texts were mutual commiserations as they missed each other's friendship. Mary shared about her new school and the fact that she was now virtually anonymous as the new girl. This was something that Mary obviously preferred over her past school. Debbie did not have that luxury which was clear from her texts as she was still being tormented by the other classmates.

There were a couple of new texts that had come in the week before Debbie was killed from her tormenters making comments and sending nasty altered pictures designed to humiliate her.

Tom made a mental note to talk to his son and ensure that when his grandkids were old enough to get cell phones that the parents would monitor their activity to guard against any similar threats and bullying. He wished he could do more to make these kids who took part in this activity understand the pain and hurt they were causing by their actions.

Maybe this was something Tom could dedicate time to after he retired, working with groups to end bullying among teenagers. He wondered if the talk with the three bullies and the parents in this case had got through to them and scared them enough to think about what they were doing.

He considered the fact that this was a major problem that was escalating in society reaching the level of virtual hate crimes. Attitudes start with small things such as the three teens saying it was all in fun until it grows into acts of hatred and prejudice. The anonymity of the social network had developed a sense of things being unreal, almost make-believe, in the minds of the perpetrators.

Debbie's iPad and laptop did not provide much more regarding answers to the questions surrounding her homicide. She had been engrossed in sites about the occult based on her internet search history even extending to her visiting sites on suicide.

There were searches on the Ouija board over the past several months and more extensive in the past month before her death, which coincided with the loss of her grandmother.

Tom wished he saw more searches of sites that could have helped Debbie both for her obvious depression and her experience of being bullied.

This was an issue currently in the news in Ontario as the recently elected provincial government, in a push towards conservative values had taken the step upon their election to scrap the school sex education program that was being taught in Ontario's public schools. The current updated version of 2015 was being rolled back to the original curriculum that was established in 1998.

The 2015 modifications had added topics like cyber-bullying, social media and LGTBQ issues.

Tom shook his head wondering how stopping the discussion and teaching on cyber bullying was going to help young teens like Debbie.

The government was arguing that they felt there was not enough parental discussion and input in the 2015 changes and would launch consultations for a new curriculum for the next school year.

Tom was a devout believer and considered himself a religious individual, but he could not understand how people could be so narrow minded and bigoted when it came to discussions about social differences that they had chosen not to believe.

Tom remembered a quote he had heard accredited to Mahatma Gandhi: "Carefully watch your thoughts, for they become your words. Manage and watch your words, for they become your actions. Consider and judge your actions, for they become your habits. Acknowledge and watch your habits, for they shall become your values. Understand and embrace your values, for they become your destiny."

Brad commented, "You are being awfully quiet, is there something that has caught your attention on the search?"

"No just thinking about this girl and what was going on in her life. Wishing someone could have helped. Anything strike you?"

"Not related to the case but this does provide details about the victims state of mind."

Tom then turned his attention to the diary to see if there was anything there that could help them.

"I want to go through this book very carefully," he commented. "There must have been a reason why the killer removed the diary and only the diary as a component of the homicide. Maybe we can identify the 'why' which could lead us to a motive and possibly a killer."

Tom opened the diary to a page from last spring.

May 4th: Dear Diary. It's been another terrible day at school. Nancy and her friends put up more posters making fun of me and Mary, calling us names. I don't know what to do or how to stop them. I wish I could just not go to school at all. Mary and I ate our lunch outside under the trees today which was nice. I don't know what I would do without Mary as my friend. Grandma is getting weaker every time we go over to the retirement home and it scares me. Mom keeps asking me if everything is okay and I say yes because I don't know how to tell them about what's happening…

He then jumped to the end of the school year.

June 25th: Dear Diary. Mary told me today that she is moving!!! Her parents are taking her to Simcoe this summer and I will not be able to be with her at school this fall. What will happen to me! I don't want to face everyone at school on my own. Please God help me."

August 15th: Dear Diary. Grandma passed away today at the retirement home, and she has left me. I no longer have my best friend; Grandma was the one person who truly loved me totally as I am. Mary's gone, Grandma's gone, and I have to go back to school all alone in a couple of weeks. Mom and Dad are talking about arrangements for the funeral. I suppose I will have to go but I don't want to, I don't want Grandma to leave me. I want to see her again, to talk to her one more time…"

Tom turned to the start of school in September.

September 7th: Dear Diary. It's worse than I thought it would be going back to school. Nancy, Sarah, and Tom are making up more things and calling me terrible names. All the other kids at school are laughing at me and snickering as I walk by. I don't know if I can take it, I don't want to go, but my parents say I must go to school. Mom and Dad went in Wednesday and talked to the principal but all he said was that it was just teenage pranks, and since they had not physically harmed me, there was nothing he could do. Mary was the lucky one to have parents who took her away from all this. I need Grandma to help me. I feel so alone…"

Finally, Tom turned to the week leading up to the homicide; he hoped to find some clue in regard to the why, so he carefully read each page which detailed Debbie's sadness and despair, chronicling the insults and the bullying on a daily basis.

The Friday, Saturday, and Sunday before the day of the homicide were the most critical for Tom since it was on those pages that forensics had found the smudged unidentified fingerprint on the Friday's entry page.

Friday September 14th: Dear Diary. Today was a professional development day for the teachers so I did not have to go to school. I went outside this morning and sat under the trees behind our house. It was nice and quiet with no one home and no one picking on me. I have decided to use the Ouija board to try and talk to grandma. I miss her so much. Mom came home and took me out for lunch which was nice. In the afternoon, I went for a walk in Springbank Park after lunch. I saw our neighbor Mr. Carson in the park this afternoon but I didn't talk to him, I think he saw me, but he didn't speak to me either. Nothing else much happened today as I have refused to read any texts or messages sent by the 'group' at school. Mary called me this evening and it was good to hear her voice. I wish every day could be like this day.

Saturday September 15th: Dear Diary. Went with Mom and Dad to the Farmers Market today and then we went to a movie. The movie was a Disney movie 'Christopher Robin.' It's been a long time since I read about the hundred-acre woods and Winnie the Pooh. The movie was about a grown-up Christopher Robin and how his childhood friends, Winnie the Pooh and Piglet, came to help him and have him help them find their lost hundred-acre woods' friends. I wish all of life could be like the hundred-acre woods where no one made fun of you or called you different. They were all just friends…"

Sunday September 16th: Dear Diary. Went to church this morning and then we went out for lunch. I miss going to visit Grandma at the retirement home. I remember how she used to keep candies in the dish by her chair so that she could give me a 'treat.' I also remember when she lived in the little house before she got ill, and we would sit on the porch and talk. Grandma always knew what to say to make me feel better. She always had time to listen to me. Tomorrow morning, I am going to try and talk to her again through the Ouija board. I'll wait till Mom and Dad go to work, and I have the house to myself. I miss Grandma so much…

Tom passed the diary to Brad and asked him to see if anything pops out to him since he could not see any new leads.

"It just doesn't make sense that the diary was the only thing the killer took unless the perpetrator was convinced that Debbie had written something in it that would incriminate him or her."

"Let me read through it and see if anything stands out to me," Brad responded.

Tom went and filled his coffee cup giving Brad time to read through the diary.

"Nothing," Brad remarked, "I don't see anything either that points us towards anyone. Maybe that's why the killer just dumped it in the park after taking it from the crime scene."

"I was thinking about one thing," Tom replied, "Debbie wrote that she and Mary had a telephone conversation on the Friday evening. Maybe if we talk to Mary again she can elaborate on their discussion and that may help."

Brad dialed the Summers' phone number but got an answering machine, so he left a message asking the Summers if they would call on Tom's direct line around 8 tomorrow morning.

Then they called it a day and left the office.

Tuesday morning came early for Tom as he woke up at 5:00 a.m. He kept thinking about the Shepherd girl and what she had gone through in her young life before the homicide happened.

He wondered how many others were out there going through the same pain and loneliness and really considered what he could do in the future to try and help individuals like Debbie.

This may be what I am called to be involved with once I retire, he mused, and the thought of actually retiring in a few weeks did not seem as bleak. Tom realized that he needed something like this where he could do some good and get involved. To make a difference.

He was ready to leave by seven and headed to the station

Following his normal morning routine, Tom filled his coffee cup and headed to his office. He spent the quiet time before the station came fully to life reviewing items on his computer.

At 7:50 a.m., Brad came into Tom's office and sat down to wait for the Summers to call. The phone rang at 8 a.m. sharp and Tom picked up the receiver.

"Tom Grant, London Police Department.

"Thank you for calling Mrs. Summers, I am going to put you on speaker so my colleague, Brad Logan can be part of the discussion as well."

Tom hit the speaker button and Brad introduced himself again and said good morning.

"Mrs. Summers we just need to ask your daughter a few more questions if you can put her on the line."

"I will place our phone on speaker as well," she replied, and the phone clicked into speaker mode.

"Hello Mary, we understand from our investigation that you and Debbie had a phone conversation on the Friday evening before she died, and we need to see if you can tell us what the two of you talked about. We are simply trying to get an understanding of what was going on that day with Debbie."

"Well," Mary started hesitantly, "It was not a big deal we just talked about school and things at home. I told her about my classes here, that no one was picking on me and she let me know that things were just as bad, maybe worse for her at our old school. We talked about her grandma and how Debbie really was missing her. That kind of stuff."

"Did Mary mention anything about what she had done or where she had gone during the day?"

"She said that she had gone for lunch with her mom and spent the day around the house. She went for a walk in the park in the afternoon. She liked to get away into the park because no one bothered her there."

"Did anything happen that she mentioned?"

"Not really, she did say she had seen her creepy neighbor Mr. Carson while she was walking in the park."

"Can you remember anything else?"

"Ya, she mentioned that Mr. Carson was walking into the bushes with two other guys that looked as creepy as him. She said they were carrying a sack of some kind. We didn't really like Mr. Carson, he was always hanging around his yard, the park, or the tree lot out back of the house. Mary told me that Mr. Carson saw her standing in the path and stared at her. That's all I can remember that we talked about."

"Thank you, Mary you have been very helpful, and we appreciate it. Have a good day at school and thank you Mrs. Summers for your assistance."

Tom and Brad thought for a few moments after they hung up before Brad made the observation, "Maybe we need to take a closer look at the neighbor here."

"Let's have him brought in for a discussion, can you have a uniformed officer bring him into the station for questioning."

"Will do." Brad left the office.

My intuition is pointing me more and more towards taking a deep dive into Mr. Carson, Tom thought to himself, picking up the phone and calling records to run a background search on Mr. Elliot Carson, currently residing on Jarvis Street in London.

It was nearly 11 in the morning when Tom was notified that Mr. Carson was in the interview room at the station. He and Brad went to the room and upon entering observed a man in blue jeans and T-shirt who appeared to be in his early thirties. He had dark black hair and was sporting a goatee and mustache of scruffy facial hair. The on-duty officer had brought him a cup of coffee which he was nursing in his hands.

"Why have I been brought here?" he demanded.

"Tom and Brad introduced themselves and advised Mr. Carson that he was being questioned in regard to the ongoing investigation of the fire and homicide that had occurred two weeks ago at his neighbor's home.

"Your people interviewed me that morning. I told them I was at home but didn't see anything before or after the time in question. I don't see what more you need from me and why you brought me down here. I have rights you know, and you can't harass me for no reason."

"I assure you Mr. Carson we have no intention of harassing you we just have a few follow up questions to ask you," Tom stated.

"We wondered if you have happened to remember any additional information that you may have missed the morning of the incident."

"Nothing." Elliott replied curtly.

"Do you make a habit of taking walks with friends in Springbank Park?" Brad queried.

"Walking in the park is not a crime the last time I checked, it's a public park. I don't need to answer to police for my actions in that regard. Anyway, I don't see what that has to do with the Shepherd killing."

"We had a report of suspicious activity in the park a few days before the incident took place and the report identified you as one of those involved," Tom commented.

"If there is something I did that you want to charge me with then charge me. Otherwise I would appreciate your squad car giving me a lift back to my home. On second thought, they can simply drop me off at the Tim Hortons coffee shop in Byron so that I can get a decent cup of coffee rather than this swell you gave me. I can walk home from there through Springbank Park."

"You're free to go Mr. Carson and we appreciate your cooperation."

Elliott Carson stood up and emptied his half-full cup of coffee into the waste bin tossing his cup in on top of it. He stomped out of the interviewed room followed by the uniformed officer that would give him a ride back to Byron.

"Pleasant fellow," Brad stated, "real class act."

"Yes, he was," Tom replied as he went to the waste bin and retrieved the discarded coffee cup. "Let's get this over to forensics and see if Mr. Carson's fingerprints have any match to the partial on the diary."

"I have asked records to run a back-ground check on Mr. Carson. In addition, I want to play a hunch and review the security tapes from the neighbors across the street when the incident occurred."

Brad went off with the cup and to arrange to retrieve the security tape.

Tom returned to his desk and mulled over the interaction with Mr. Carson. Something felt odd in regards to their prior guest and he intended to find out why.

It was later in the day when Brad returned to Tom's office with the security tape.

"Report from forensics is here, the fingerprint smudge on the diary was an inconclusive match because of the smudging and could not be positively linked to Mr. Carson. I have asked them to run Mr. Carson's fingerprints against the criminal database just to see if our friend has any criminal history that we may not be aware of."

"Well done," Tom remarked, "The background check on our Mr. Carson came back empty as the records don't show any information on an Elliott Carson in London or anywhere else as far as it relates to our new suspect's description."

"Oh, so we are calling him a suspect now?" Brad questioned.

"In the least, he definitely rises to the level of a 'person of interest.'" Tom replied.

The two of them reviewed the security tape.

"I don't see how this helps us," commented Brad, "I don't see Mr. Carson in the tape at all."

"That's what is bothering me," mused Tom, "Here he is living next door to the Shepherds, hears the emergency sirens, has to have seen all the activity in the street, and yet he is the only neighbor who does not come out and investigate. We know he was home because he told the investigating officer he was there during the time of the crime in his initial crime scene interview.

"Would you simply sit in your house when all this commotion is going on a few hundred meters from your home?

"Let's regroup tomorrow after forensics finishes the fingerprint search and see where we are at regarding Mr. Carson."

It was Wednesday morning of week three of the investigation when Tom and Brad reconvened in Tom's office.

Forensics had obtained a match on the fingerprints, and they belonged to a Mr. Elliott Brown, age thirty-two. His last known address had been eleven months earlier in a suburb of Toronto.

He had a criminal record for petty drug and robbery charges and had been arrested eight years ago for aggravated assault. The assault had been considered egregious and involved a knife which resulted in a three-year term in prison at Millhaven Institution, a maximum-security facility.

After his release, he had been arrested for drug trafficking which had provided him another two year stay in the custody of the prison system.

"This is looking more and more like someone we need to dig into, but we don't have enough probable cause or evidence to even get a search warrant for his home," Tom remarked.

"Let's put Mr. Carson i.e. Brown under surveillance and see if we can find any unusual activity regarding what appears to be his routine visits to Springbank Park."

The following two days did not bring in any new leads and Tom and Brad were now concentrating their attention on Mr. Brown. Undercover officers were keeping the home of Mr. Brown under surveillance, and on one occasion on the Thursday afternoon had followed him discreetly through the park to the Tim Hortons in downtown Byron a short 30-minute walk from his home.

There he met with two other gentlemen and photos of the meeting had been sent to forensics to see if facial recognition could identify his companions.

Tom knew that this was a long shot and could not continue with this level of use of manpower for very long, but he was hoping for a break.

CHAPTER FOUR: WEEK FIVE

It was Monday morning the first day of October, the start of the fourth week since the Shepherd's homicide.

Tom was convinced that Elliott Brown was the prime suspect but without tangible motive or any probable cause, they could not act upon their suspicions.

All they could do was to keep looking and hope for a break.

Tom and Brad were called into the deputy chief's office at 1:15 in the afternoon.

Deputy Chief Jones asked them to provide a status update on the Shepherd case, and Tom and Brad described their findings, the details of the investigation, and the reasoning for why they were now concentrating on Elliott Brown.

The deputy chief sympathized with the concerns that had been raised regarding the in-school cyber bullying and advised them to talk to the Community Policing Section. Community Policing can follow up to ensure that the teens involved have learned their lesson and also emphasize the criminal aspect of cyber and in person bullying in the schools.

"We need to find a way to get through to these kids in the elementary school system, so they stop the bullying before it starts. Heaven knows with kids having cell phones and computers as young as four and five it's not an easy task, but we need to work with the schools and parents to teach these kids during their formative years.

"The way it is today there is just too much negative influence around and it must be addressed not by the police, or teachers, or parents alone but as a concerted effort by all parties with trained resources."

"That's enough of my soap box speech for today. Regarding the Shepherd's case, I can keep Mr. Brown under surveillance for the balance of this week but if nothing substantive emerges after that, I will have to realign those resources. You will just need to keep working the Shepherd's case in tandem as I need to assign you to a new case that needs us to follow up on urgently.

"Over the course of this weekend, we have had eight cases of opioid overdoses. Fortunately, four have been treated and will survive but four have died.

"The forensics team is telling us that, based on the residue traces provided by the emergency responders, there appears to be a particularly lethal type of fentanyl out there on the streets. The fentanyl has been mixed with heroin which has caused the strength to be enhanced resulting in multiple overdoses that we are aware of. Two of those who survived had used the safe injection site for taking the drugs and the staff were able to counteract the overdose with naloxone and oxygen. One had injected in a location downtown but other individuals with them had called emergency services that were able to respond quickly with the same naloxone counter treatment. The final case that survived had injected in a private home that had another person present. The individual present had contacted emergency response. The four fatalities did not have naloxone kits at the scene, and there was no call to emergency responders to prevent the resulting overdose deaths.

"Here are the initial attending officers' reports on the four deaths and the four that survived including the background information that could be obtained on each one. The autopsy reports will be received shortly as the medical examiner is doing a quick turnaround to verify cause of death. I don't need to tell you that we have to get a handle on where and who is distributing this poison as quickly as possible before this results in a mass of cases and potentially deaths. The media relations department has issued a statement to the press to try and raise awareness in the public. The safe injection site run by the Middlesex London Health Unit has workers talking to everyone out on the street that they can in conjunction with those organizations that are out interacting with the homeless population."

Tom responded, "Will do Chief Jones."

Tom and Brad left the deputy chief's office and headed back to Tom's office to regroup and strategize.

"The first thing we need to do is try and contact the four individuals who survived and see if we can get a handle on the source. Let's review the emergency responders and responding officers' reports on the two that involved primary responders and the Middlesex London Health Unit reports on the two individuals that were treated at the Safe Injection Site along with the emergency responders that transported them to hospital."

Brad made copies of the initial reports so they could read through the reports and make notes for follow-up. They would each read the reports separately so they could compare notes and see if there was anything different that stuck out to them individually.

Brad left for his desk and Tom settled in to read his copies.

The first set of reports were on the four who had died from the opioid overdose injections.

Responding Officer Report: Case 251 Officer J. Black
Victim: John Simpson age 22, homeless – no fixed address.

Description: Dark brown hair and beard, blue eyes, weight approximately 63 kilograms, height approximately 1.7 meters.

Date and time: Friday September 28th 10:30 p.m.

I was on uniformed patrol, driving on King Street near the corner of King and Richmond when I noticed an individual lying in the entranceway to a closed storefront. I engaged my cruiser lights and proceeded to go over and check on the individual. Upon examination of the scene, I noticed a discharged needle lying beside the victim and checked for life signs before calling into dispatch for an emergency response ambulance. I also noted the presence of vomit beside the body.

Emergency responders arrived at 10:38 p.m. and upon examination verified that the person was deceased. They declared the subject dead at the scene.

The body was taken by ambulance to the forensics pathology unit for coroner's autopsy.

As attending officer, I took photographs of the scene for inclusion in my report prior to the body removal.

By standers who had come to the scene during the emergency response identified the name of the victim and stated they were not aware of any home address for the victim.

End of report. Signed Officer J. Brown.

Tom continued to the second report.

Responding Officer Report: Case 298 Officer A. Henderson

Victim: Eric Peters age 25, homeless – no fixed address.

Description: Black hair, no facial hair, brown eyes, weight approximately 74 kilograms, height approximately 1.8 meters.

Date and time: Saturday September 29th 7:00 a.m.

I was on uniformed patrol on Talbot Street in the vicinity of Dundas and Talbot by Budweiser Gardens.

I noted an individual who was curled up on the curb and proceeded to stop my cruiser and engage my cruiser alert lights.

Upon approaching the victim, I noted the presence of vomit on his chin and sleeve, and there was a discarded needle visible under his left arm.

I checked for life signs and could not detect any. I called into dispatch for emergency services which arrived at the scene at 7:10 a.m.

Emergency responders attended to the body but determined there were no vital signs and declared the individual deceased at the scene.

Emergency responders took the body to the forensics pathology unit to await the corner.

I took photographs of the body and the scene before the body was removed by emergency responders.

By standers who were in the vicinity of the scene during the emergency response identified the name of the victim and stated they were not aware of any home address for the victim.

End of report: Signed Officer A. Henderson

Responding Officer Report: Case 302 Officer A. Henderson

Victim: Nancy Taylor age 32, homeless – no fixed address.

Description: Blonde hair, blue eyes, weight approximately 48 kilograms, height approximately 1.6 meters.

Date and time: Saturday September 29th 8:45 a.m.

A call was received at dispatch from a store owner on Dundas Street just east of the Adelaide Street intersection.

The store owner had arrived to open his business and found a body of a female slumped in the store's front doorway.

Dispatch had also contacted emergency responders to attend the scene.

I arrived at approximately the same time as the arrival of the emergency response ambulance at 8:52 a.m.

Emergency responders engaged with the victim but determined there were no life signs and declared the victim to be dead at the scene.

I noted there was a used needle on the sidewalk in front of where the victim was curled up in the doorway of the shop.

I took photographs of the scene and the emergency responders removed the body and transported it to the forensics pathology unit for the arrival of the coroner.

Interviewed store owner Mr. Kim who verified that he had arrived at the store through the back entrance at 8:30 in the morning where he proceeded to prepare the store to open for 9:00 a.m. When he walked to the front of the store and prepared to unlock the front door, he observed the body of the young women on the front doorway stoop.

He had opened the door and checked to see if she was asleep but when she did not respond he called 911.

Store owner Mr. Kim said he had seen the victim around the area several times in the past and that she was part of the street people that frequented the vicinity.

Store owner was able to identify the name of the victim from prior conversations he had with her, but stated he was not aware of any home address for the victim.

End of report: Signed Officer A. Henderson

Responding Officer Report: Case 312 Officer S. Jones

Victim: Tom Sanders age 33, resident of London and Middlesex Affordable Housing apartment building, 1194 Commissioners Road W.

Description: Greying hair, brown eyes, weight approximately 82 kilograms, height approximately 1.7 meters.

Date and time: Saturday September 29th 10:15 a.m.

A call was received at dispatch from a cell phone, caller identified herself as Carrie Anderson, resident of the apartment building at 1194 Commissioners Road W.

Caller stated there was a body in the park and that the person was not moving or responding. She stated she recognized the individual as a resident in her apartment building located across the road from Springbank Park on Commissioners Road.

Ms. Anderson was asked to remain at the scene and emergency response would arrive shortly.

Dispatch directed me and emergency response to proceed to the scene located just inside the park past the parking area accessed by West Springbank Park Gate. Caller had indicated that she would stay beside the internal access road inside the park and show them where the body was located in the woods.

I arrived at the scene at 10:25 a.m. Emergency responders arrived within two minutes after my arrival.

We accompanied Ms. Anderson into the grassy section of the park surrounded by mature trees where we located the victim sitting on the ground, leaning against a tree stump. There was a discarded needle on the ground beside where the victim was sitting.

Emergency responders checked Mr. Sanders for vital signs but found none declaring that he was deceased at the scene.

After I photographed and documented the scene, the emergency responders transported the body to forensics pathology unit to await the coroner.

I interviewed Ms. Anderson and she verified the identity of Mr. Sanders and that he was a fellow resident of the London and Middlesex Housing apartment building situated at 1194 Commissioners Road W across from the entrance to the park.

She advised me that she has been a resident for the past year and had met Mr. Sanders on various occasions in the apartment building hallway, mailbox location in the lobby, and at some social occasions the building manager had held at the building.

She confirmed that she did not know him very well, just enough to say hello and talk briefly in passing.

Ms. Anderson stated that she had gone for a walk in the park this morning entering across from her apartment building and walking along the internal road known as Flint Lane until she reached the area in question. She was cutting through the trees to reach a path that lead down to Rivers Edge Drive in order to sit on the park benches overlooking the Thames River and the Dam. As she was walking, she noticed Mr. Sanders sitting on the ground against the tree and decided to go over and say good morning but when she approached him he was non-responsive, so she called 911.

Ms. Anderson stated that she had not seen any other persons or any suspicious activity in the park when she arrived.

End of report: Signed Officer S. Jones

Tom considered how sad and preventable these four deaths had been, isolated and alone without anyone to assist them. He had been part of a training class that had informed the officers that opioid deaths were generally preventable in the cases where there was someone else nearby to notify emergency response. The signs of an opioid overdose generally allowed for time to respond when identified quickly. He was also aware that the drug naloxone was available at no cost to 'at risk' individuals and their caregivers and works within minutes of administration to counteract the opioid.

Tom decided to refresh his knowledge and proceeded to look up information on opioid that was plaguing his city, as well as naloxone.

The Government of Canada website[15] provided a good source of concise and pertinent information.

About Opioids:

Opioids are drugs with pain relieving properties that are used primarily to treat pain.

Opioids can also induce euphoria (feeling high), which gives them the potential to be used improperly.

Opioids can be prescribed medications:

- *codeine*
- *fentanyl*
- *morphine*
- *oxycodone*
- *hydromorphone*
- *medical heroin*

Opioids are intended to treat pain.

Problematic opioid use:

Opioids have the potential for problematic use because they can produce euphoria (feeling high).

---

15 www.canada.ca/en/health-canada/services/substance-use/problematic-drug-use/opioids

When people think about problematic opioid use, they often think about when someone takes an illegally produced or obtained opioid, such as:

☐ *heroin*

☐ *fentanyl*

Problematic use of opioids also includes when you:

☐ *use an opioid medicine improperly, such as:*

o *taking more than is prescribed*

o *taking it at the wrong time*

☐ *use an opioid medicine that was not prescribed for you*

Substance use disorder:

When someone is affected by substance use disorder or addiction, they crave the drug and continue using it despite the harmful effects. The drug becomes the focus of their feelings, thoughts, and activities.

Opioid use disorder also changes the brain and the body in ways that can make it hard to stop using. This is because the body gets used to a regular supply of the drug. If you stop using the drug, or lower your dose quickly, you will likely experience withdrawal symptoms.

Overdose:

An overdose can happen when you take too much of an opioid. Opioids affect the part of your brain that controls your breathing. When you take more opioids than your body can handle, your breathing slows. This can lead to unconsciousness and even death.

Signs and symptoms of an opioid overdose:

Recognize the signs and symptoms of an overdose, including:

☐ *difficulty in walking, talking and staying awake*

- ☐ *blue lips or nails*
- ☐ *very small pupils*
- ☐ *cold and clammy skin*
- ☐ *dizziness and confusion*
- ☐ *extreme drowsiness*
- ☐ *choking, gurgling or snoring sounds*
- ☐ *slow, weak or no breathing*
- ☐ *inability to wake up, even when shaken or shouted at*

Reduce the risk:

If you use opioids, you can reduce your risk of overdose or death by:

- ☐ *not using alone*
- ☐ *knowing your tolerance (how much you can take)*
- ☐ *having a naloxone kit available, and knowing how to use it*
- ☐ *using a small amount of an opioid first to check the strength*
- ☐ *not taking opioids with alcohol or other drugs (unless prescribed by your doctor)*

In his researching the background information on opioids, Tom was struck by the one statement.

It is rare for someone to die immediately from an overdose. When people survive, it's because someone was there to respond.

That was something that struck Tom as he was reading the case notes. The four deaths this past weekend from overdoses were those individuals who had been alone, not at the safe injection site, with a friend or at home with other people like the other four.

Tom then went to the Province of Ontario web site[16] to refresh his information on the use of naloxone to prevent death from an overdose.

What naloxone does:

Naloxone (pronounced na-LOX-own, also known by the brand name Narcan) is a drug that can temporarily reverse an opioid overdose. Opioids are drugs that are usually used to treat pain, but some people use opioids to get high.

When someone overdoses on opioids, their breathing either slows or stops completely. If used right away, naloxone can help them breathe normally and regain consciousness. Naloxone can either be injected or given as a nasal spray.

Who can get a free naloxone kit:

You are eligible for a free kit if you are:

- ☐ *a current opioid user or a past user who is at risk of using again*

- ☐ *a family member, friend or other person able to help someone at risk of an opioid overdose*

- ☐ *a client of a needle syringe program or hepatitis C program*

- ☐ *newly released from a correctional facility*

Tom noted that there were over 125 pharmacies and community based organizations in the greater London area that dispensed and distributed the free kits. Those locations also trained the individual recipient on how to use the kit if needed.

Tom also noted that the naloxone was a temporary intervention and that the individual still needed to receive medical treatment.

Tom then turned his attention to the corners reports on the four fatalities that had arrived during his review of the police reports.

16 www.ontario.ca/page/get-naloxone-kits-free

A coroner or forensic pathologist must answer five questions when investigating a death:

- ☐ Who (identity of the deceased)

- ☐ When (date of death)

- ☐ Where (location of death)

- ☐ How (medical cause of death)

- ☐ By what means (natural causes, accident, homicide, suicide or undetermined)

All four of the reports were basically identical except for the individual case details.

Autopsy report 1025. Coroner's signature

- ☐ Identity of the deceased: John Simpson

- ☐ Date of Death: September 28th 10:30 p.m.

- ☐ Location of death: near the corner of King and Richmond

- ☐ Medical cause of death: Asphyxiation due to opioid overdoes

- ☐ Means: Accidental

Autopsy report 1031. Coroner's signature

- ☐ Identity of the deceased: Eric Peters

- ☐ Date of Death: September 29th 7:00 a.m.

- ☐ Location of death: Vicinity of Dundas and Talbot by Budweiser Gardens

- ☐ Medical cause of death: Asphyxiation due to opioid overdoes

- ☐ Means: Accidental

Autopsy report 1039. Coroner's signature

- ☐ Identity of the deceased: Nancy Taylor

- ☐ Date of death: September 29th 8:45 a.m.

- ☐ Location of death: Dundas Street just east of Adelaide Street

- ☐ Medical cause of death: Asphyxiation due to opioid overdoes

- ☐ Means: Accidental

Autopsy report 1042. Coroner's signature

- ☐ Identity of the deceased: Tom Sanders

- ☐ Date of death: September 29th 10:15 a.m.

- ☐ Location of death: Springbank Park, in wooded area by west gate entrance

- ☐ Medical cause of death: Asphyxiation due to opioid overdoes

- ☐ Means: Accidental

There were basically no witnesses to the time of death.

The only persons with information to add were the individuals who found the deceased, store owner Mr. Kim and Ms. Carrie Anderson who lived in the same building as Mr. Sanders.

Tom made note of the contact and address information for Ms. Anderson, so he and Brad could do a follow up interview. She may have seen someone coming or going in the building with Mr. Sanders.

Next it was time to review the reports on those who had survived.

Responding Officer Report: Case 231 Officer B. Lieder

Person Involved: Marion Casey, age 39, resident of apartment building located at 750 Wonderland Road, London

Description: Brown hair, brown eyes, weight 58 kilograms, height 1.6 meters.

Date and time: Friday September 28th 8:15 p.m.

A call was received at dispatch from a cell phone, caller identified herself as Evelyn Casey, resident of the apartment building at 750 Wonderland Road, London.

Caller stated that her daughter Marion was unresponsive in her bedroom and Ms. Casey could not wake her. She indicated that her daughter was breathing irradicably and making odd noises.

Dispatch asked if there were any signs or history of drug use. Ms. Casey responded there were no signs she could see but her daughter has had a problem with drug use in the past.

Ms. Casey was asked to remain on the line with dispatch and emergency response would arrive shortly.

Dispatch advised they had directed emergency response to proceed to the scene and that the call involved a potential drug overdose. Caller would stay on the line and provide the responders access to the apartment building when they arrived.

I arrived at the scene at 8:25 p.m. Emergency responders had arrived shortly before my arrival and were proceeding to the apartment unit.

Emergency responders checked Ms. Marion Casey's vital signs. Her breathing was distressed, and the responders located a used needle on the floor under the side of the bed. They determined that she was suffering from an opioid overdose based on the signs and symptoms of the individual. Responders administered naloxone and oxygen, and the patient began to respond quickly. The patient was then transported to St. Joseph's Hospital for follow up treatment.

I interviewed Ms. Evelyn Casey, the individual's mother. Ms. Casey was extremely upset and broke down several times. I asked her if there was a family member she could contact, and she phoned a neighbor in the apartment building who advised they would be right there. Ms. Casey stated that her daughter had struggled with drug addiction most of her adult life and had been recently in rehabilitation treatment. She was not aware that her daughter had slipped back into her old habits. She stated that her daughter had been attending Narcotics Anonymous for the past six months and had been doing so well. She confided that her daughter's moods had been good, and she could not understand why Marion would have started to use drugs again.

A neighbor Elizabeth Hancock arrived at this point and said she would stay with Ms. Casey and take her to the hospital to check on her daughter.

End of report: Signed Officer B. Lieder

Responding Officer Report: Case 242 Officer B. Lieder

Person Involved: Bridgett Collins, age 30, resident of no fixed address, London

Description: Dark hair, green eyes, weight 62 kilograms, height 1.7 meters.

Date and time: Friday September 28th 10:58 p.m.

A call was received at dispatch from a cell phone, caller identified himself as a friend of the individual but would not provide his name.

Caller stated that she was hanging out near Richmond Street in Victoria Park when he came upon a friend, Bridgett Collins, lying on the ground in the park close to the cenotaph at the corner of Wellington and Dufferin. She was breathing badly, and he could not wake her. He knew that she had obtained some opioid early in the evening when they had been talking.

Dispatch asked if the caller had access to a naloxone kit and he advised no. Dispatch asked if the caller would provide his name, and he said no as he had used a different drug and did not want to be arrested or hassled. He said he would keep an eye on the patient until emergency response arrived, but he was not staying to talk with them.

Dispatch directed emergency response to proceed to the scene and that the call involved a suspected drug overdose.

I arrived at the scene at 11:03 p.m. Emergency responders arrived basically at the same time.

Emergency responders checked Ms. Collins's vital signs. Her breathing was distressed, and the responders located a used needle on the ground. Based on the needle and the information obtained from the unidentified caller, they determined that she was suffering from an opioid overdose based on the signs and symptoms of the individual. Responders administered naloxone and oxygen, and the patient began to respond within a couple of minutes. The patient was then transported to St. Joseph's Hospital for follow up treatment.

As indicated, the caller had left the scene before the time of the emergency responder's arrival and was not available for interview. No one was observed in the park area at the time of arrival, but a crowd gathered shortly after we arrived and were observing the incident.

I approached the crowd that had gathered and asked if anyone could provide any information on the incident, but everyone stated they had been attracted by the sirens and lights and had no knowledge of the incident.

None of the bystanders could provide a home address for Ms. Collins.

End of report: Signed officer B Leiter

Tom made a note to have patrol locate Ms. Bridgett Collins and also for him and Brad to visit with the Caseys for follow up interviews.

The final two case reports involved the two incidents that had occurred at the London's Temporary Overdose Prevention Site located at 186 King Street in London.

Tom remembered the discussions that had taken place when the temporary site had opened in February of this year.

The site is being run by the Middlesex London Health Unit and was the first temporary overdose prevention site opened in Ontario. The medical officer had commented at the time:

"Having people injecting in a safer and contained environment is good for keeping people alive, it's good for neighborhoods, there's less needle waste on the streets, less public injecting behaviors, it's a really good thing for everyone."

News reports recently had stated that the temporary site was being funded through to October by the provincial government. Under the previous provincial government of Ontario, cities had been moving ahead with plans to identify permanent sites, holding public meetings, etc.

Tom had seen the news reports with numerous quotes from individuals who started by stating they were in favor of the injection prevention sites and the philosophy but for every site selected they would go on to state that it was too populated an area, too close to sensitive properties, etc., ending with the statement that the health unit needs to find a suitable site but my area is not the right site.

Tom remembered discussions he had heard since the 1970s about locations for municipal waste disposal which had always ended with what was referred to as the NIMBY phenomena (Not In My Back Yard).

The newly elected provincial government had placed a moratorium on any and all new Overdose Prevention Sites in the province 'until further study could be undertaken regarding the value of the sites and if they actually prevented deaths.'

Tom sighed and wondered why politics had to get in the way of saving lives but that was reality.

Responding Officer Report: Case 312 Officer A. Henderson

First person involved: Allan Jones age 42, homeless – no fixed address.

Description: Black hair, brown eyes, weight 59 kilograms, height 1.8 meters.

Second person involved: Samantha Lester age 19, apartment, 435 Grey Street, London.

Description: Blond hair, blue eyes, weight 54 kilograms, height 1.55 meters.

Date and time: Saturday September 29th 11:05 a.m.

A call was received at dispatch from the London Overdose Prevention Site located at 186 King Street, London.

The attendant at the site had called 911 due to two individuals who had displayed symptoms of opioid overdose within the past twenty minutes at the site.

Dispatch notified me and had also contacted emergency responders to the scene.

I arrived just after the arrival of the emergency response ambulance at 11:12 a.m.

Attendants at the site had administered naloxone and oxygen when the individuals had become non-responsive. Emergency responders checked vital signs and noted that the individuals of concern were responding to the treatment administered by the site attendants.

Emergency response prepared and transported the two individuals to St. Joseph's Hospital for medical follow up.

I moved my cruiser down the street and disengaged my emergency lights before proceeding back to the site to interview the attendant who had administered the initial dose of naloxone. We met in the back office at the Overdoes Prevention Site in accordance with established protocol so as not to discourage any other clients from accessing the site.

The attendant stated that the two individuals had come into the site separately approximately five minutes apart and then proceeded to the self-injection booths. The clean needles and disposal of used needles is handled by the user in the booth area after which they proceed to the waiting room area. Protocol has the user remain in the site for at least 30 minutes to ensure no harmful effects are being felt by the individual.

Both of the users had started to show symptoms of potential concern, so the attendant has asked them what they had used which they verified was Heroine mixed with opioid fentanyl. Both were becoming unresponsive to outside stimulus, face pale and clammy, and their breathing was becoming slow and shallow. When the first individual displayed loss of consciousness, the attendant advised the other staff member to call 911 and then administered naloxone to the patients. The attendant also administered oxygen.

End of report: Signed Officer A. Henderson

Tom went online to research the issues involved with mixing fentanyl with heroin as was the case with the drug in question with these cases.

The research provided these facts.

Fentanyl is 100 times more powerful then heroin but mixing fentanyl with heroin intensifies the potency and the addictiveness. The normal occurrence is that street dealers selling heroin use the fentanyl to create more potent heroin to enhance the affects and make their clients more dependent on their supply.

Just this past March in the City of Hamilton Ontario, there was a rash of overdoses in heroin users that were taking a street drug called 'Purple Heroin' which had been mixed or cut with fentanyl. The report went on to state that in the City of Hamilton in 2017 for the 10-month period from January to October seventy people had died because of opioid related causes.

In the current instance in London, the dealer was mixing fentanyl into the heroine, creating a lethal strength combination. This left Tom wondering if the mixture was due to ignorance or deliberate on the part of the dealer

Tom thought back to 1971 when he had entered the Sociology Degree (Criminology) program at Western University in London. He had met Ann that past year in the Town of Simcoe, and they had been a couple ever since. After his first year at Western, they had decided to get married and move in together in London at the start of the fall semester of his second year.

They had a small family wedding in June of that year and began their 46 years of married life.

That summer in Simcoe the drug scene had hit the community but back then, the drugs of choice were smoking marijuana and 'dropping' acid which was taking Lysergic Acid Diethylamide (LSD) pills in order to get the feeling of being high. Heroin was known but not prevalent and the use of 'speed' was considered the hard drug. Speed was a methamphetamine and when taken by needle gave the user a manic high sensation.

Overdosing on LSD in those days was more in line with getting too 'high' and 'freaking out' on the hallucinations. The general treatment was to observe the individual and keep them from doing themselves harm while they worked through the high.

Tom and Ann had friends who had been involved but there was not the rash of overdoses that were prevalent today. The big issue was the number of teenage suicides and feelings of isolation which had not really changed in the 46 years since but with the increase in online bullying, the problem had gotten worse.

Tom and Ann were part of a group in 1970 that formed a support organization in the town called 'Project Help' to establish a drop-in coffee house for youth to come and talk and be together. This provided an accepting and safe environment for the youth to meet and in the event that they were high, a place they could be with others.

Tom remembered a poem entitled *You* he had read recently that described the LSD age which seemed to have been a gentler and less deadly time.

With the darkness comes the light
The stars like crystals shining bright.
To stare upon the sky and see
How bright they shine in their darkened sea
Of colored blackness float.

Walking with mind reeling so
The plants about you seem to grow
And shrink and move and soon you'll find
Their shape and movement is your mind
You're grooving.

Music softly drifts into your head,
Grasping you, holding you in its beats stead.
Slowly it drones on into the night
Colors about you dance with the flight
And your soul is free.

With eyes of perception upon small things you gaze,
Things unnoticed upon your straight days
Like a shaft of light, or dew on a rose
A bug on a leaf, a lawn newly mowed
Nature is you.

The universe and you are joined in the night

You feel yourself linked with the bird in its flight
Peace of mind is yours as the colors burst forth
You feel reawakened as a child at its birth
You are you.[17]

That July when the tobacco transient workers from Quebec and other places arrived in Simcoe to work the tobacco harvest there was an issue. The late spring had delayed the tobacco crop and the workers had arrived two weeks early. They had no places to stay or eat since the Salvation Army generally ran the soup kitchens and provided food until the harvest started. The Salvation Army was not going to open for meals for that two-week period.

Tom on behalf of Project Help had approach the pastor and elders of the Community of Christ Church in Simcoe, as Ann's family was part of the small congregation. Ironically, the small white church building was located on the street Tom had grown up on and had a small kitchen and fellowship hall downstairs that would sit around 50 people.

The neighborhood was a quiet residential street.

When Tom approached the elders and asked if they could use the basement fellowship hall to feed between 300 and 400 people a day for two meals he was not sure how they would react.

The pastor and elders had not hesitated and agreed to trust Tom and the volunteers, so Project Help ran a soup kitchen for 10 days that summer from the basement of that little white church.

Tom often accredited his conversion to his wife's denomination as the result of their willingness and compassion and had been a member ever since.

After completing a three-year degree in Criminology at Western, Tom had decided to pursue a career in law enforcement so he took the Police Officer Diploma Program and joined the London Police Force.

---

17 Flights of Poetry, Ronald Rowbottom, ISBN 9781947353336, Austin Macauley Publishers.

Tom concluded his walk down memory lane and made a further follow up note to contact the Overdose Prevention Site and arrange for the attendant to come into the station for a follow up interview. The police were trying hard to work with the site and not violate the confidentiality that was mandatory if drug users were going to be willing to come to the site and use the services.

Tom reviewed his notes and then called Brad into his office, "Brad, here are the autopsies on the four casualties involved in this weekend drug overdoses for your review. In regards to the survivors, I need you to contact the Overdose Prevention Center and get the name of the attendant who was involved. Arrange for that individual to come into the office tomorrow morning for a follow up interview.

"In addition, contact uniformed patrol and see if they can locate the homeless individuals who were involved at the safe injection site, Bridgett Collins and Allan Jones, and have them brought in for a follow up interview.

"I will contact the other two individuals that we have home addresses on and we will arrange to interview them.

"We need to try and put an identity on whoever is pedaling this fentanyl mixture out on the streets and make sure we are ahead of any more incidents if possible."

"Will do," Brad replied.

"Come into my office tomorrow morning after you finish and let's discuss our next actions and plan our interviews," Tom remarked.

Tom sat at his desk and contemplated everything he had read before he gathered his hat and coat and headed home for the evening.

The next morning, Tom was enjoying his morning coffee when he received a report from the surveillance team that was watching Elliot Brown.

Yesterday afternoon, Mr. Brown (Carson) had been observed leaving his home by way of the back woodlot where he proceeded to cross Springbank

Drive and enter Springbank Park. He was observed carrying a small parcel wrapped in brown paper. The surveillance team followed Mr. Brown (Carson) who met up with two other gentlemen in the park and proceeded to go with them into a more heavily wooded area. Surveillance took a photograph of Mr. Brown (Carson) and the two unidentified individuals.

An electronic copy of the photograph had been forwarded to Tom's email account.

Surveillance could not observe what occurred in the wooded area but the trio emerged approximately 20 minutes later with one of the unidentified subjects carrying the small parcel Mr. Brown (Carson) had brought to the park. Mr. Brown (Carson) proceeded to walk along the walkway heading towards the west gate entrance at the far end of the park off Commissioners Road while the other two had headed towards the parking area off the east gate on Springbank Drive.

The surveillance team had separated and followed both groups. Mr. Brown proceeded to the Byron Tim Hortons on Commissioners Road; the other two individuals had walked to the bus stop on Springbank Road by the parking entrance. They boarded the city bus at the bus stop on the far side of Springbank Road heading towards the downtown area.

Tom printed a copy of the photograph for inclusion in the Shepherd's case file.

The telephone rang and when Tom answered, it was Brad. The attendant from the injection site would be stopping in at 11:00 this morning. Uniformed patrol believed they have located the two homeless individuals and would verify this sometime this afternoon. They would notify when they had been found and bring them to the station for interviews.

At 11:00 a.m. sharp, Eddie Singleton arrived at the station. Eddie was the attendant who had been on duty at the time of the overdoses at the safe injection site.

Tom and Brad met Mr. Singleton in the interview room.

"Good Morning Mr. Singleton," Tom started, "I am Detective Tom Grant, and this is Detective Brad Logan. We are investigating the large number of overdoses that occurred over the weekend from the fentanyl laced heroin."

"Ya, there was some really bad stuff being distributed out there," Eddie remarked, continuing:

"The Middlesex London Health Unit immediately had the word put out on the street through individuals we know and cooperating agencies and groups that a lethal concentration was being packaged and sold.

"Fortunately, we have not heard about any additional cases that have been reported since Saturday after the word went out."

"That is extremely good news," Brad remarked. "Can you describe in detail what occurred on Saturday?"

"I basically described everything to the attending officer that day and we appreciate the sensitivity that the officer showed during his report taking."

"Did either of the individuals happen to mention who they had bought the fentanyl from?" Tom queried.

"No, our protocol is that we don't ask. But I have heard random comments about a couple of individuals who have popped up a lot in street talk. They are relatively new to the scene downtown. Their names are Pete or Peter Carruthers and the other one goes by John Smith."

"Could you describe or identify these gentlemen?"

"No, I can't say I can, I have never seen them as such, nor have I heard about them coming into the injection site. Just heard small talk by clients about the two of them in downtown London. The jest of the conversation seemed to be that they are individuals that could supply."

"Thank you Mr. Singleton, we appreciate your cooperation and help. If you hear any other information that could assist us in this case please let us know. Personally, I want you to know that I support your efforts to help these individuals," Tom commented.

Eddie left the station, and Tom and Brad considered what to do next.

Tom called the home phone numbers for Samantha Lester and Marion Casey.

Mrs. Casey answered and said that her daughter was home and resting but was leaving to attend a Narcotics Anonymous meeting that afternoon, so Tom arranged to come over to visit them at 10:00 the next morning. Tom mentioned the fact that it was good that Marion had reconnected with the support group and hoped everything went well.

"This was a bad scare and maybe Marion can get herself back together," Mrs. Casey stated but Tom could hear the desperation and hesitation in her voice.

"We will see you in the morning." Tom finished the conversation.

Tom then called Samantha Lester.

"Hello."

"Good Morning Ms. Lester, I am Detective Tom Grant and we are the investigating detectives regarding the number of opioid overdoses from fentanyl that occurred over this past weekend. I understand you had experienced an overdose which resulted in your hospitalization overnight Saturday, and we would like to interview you."

"No way, I don't want to talk to the police, and I am not coming down to the police station. I don't want anything more to do with this. The Safe Injection Site was not supposed to release my name."

"Ms. Lester, the Safe Injection Site did not release your name. We received your contact information from the emergency responders and hospital."

"I don't have to talk to you."

"Ms. Lester, we can either arrange to come and meet you at your apartment or we can have a patrol car come and bring you to the station. Whichever you prefer."

"I don't want police arriving at my apartment and making me a spectacle for all my neighbors. If I have to meet with you, I will come down to the station myself."

"That will be fine, do you know where to come?"

"Yes."

"Then ask for Detective Tom Grant, when and what time will you be here?"

"I'll come this afternoon and be there around two o'clock."

"That would be fine Ms. Lester but make sure you come, or we will have to have our uniformed officers find you."

After he hung up, Tom made the comment to Brad that this will likely be an uncooperative respondent, the chances of getting the dealer from her will likely be small, but it's worth a try.

"Do you think we are going to have to have uniforms go find her?" Brad asked.

"Not sure but we will know this afternoon. Time to grab lunch."

After lunch Tom noted that his desk phone was blinking a message. It was the deputy chief asking Tom to call him.

Tom dialed the deputy chief's number, "It's Tom, you needed to speak to me?"

"Yes, I have a favor to ask. The Ward 10 City Councilor is holding a monthly constituents meeting tomorrow evening at the Civic Gardens Center building on Springbank Drive. Ironically, her scheduled presentation and discussion is on the opioid crisis in London, and she has a representative from the Middlesex London Health Unit coming to present. Since the Civic Gardens Center is part of Springbank Park and with the news articles about the overdose deaths including the one in Springbank Park which is in her riding, she has asked that the police have someone attend.

"As the lead detective on this, I would like you to attend on behalf of the force, give a brief update on the investigation and answer any questions that may come up regarding police involvement."

"Not really my specialty," Tom replied.

"I understand but based on the circumstances you are the best person we have to represent us and be a part of this meeting."

"Okay, I'll try but some of my answers may be pretty vague just in case there is any negative feedback."

"Not a problem and by the way Tom, don't be surprised if there are reporters there and you get questioned about the ongoing Shepherd's homicide since it's just down the street from that scene."

"Thanks for the heads up."

Tom dropped the phone into the receiver and sat back in his chair.

This was not something he needed dropped onto his lap with the two ongoing investigations and the fact he was just over four weeks from retirement, but he resolved himself to the situation by stating it is what it is.

At 2:30 in the afternoon, a sullen and visually uncooperative Samantha Lester was sitting in the interview room when Tom and Brad entered.

"Ms. Lester, my name is Detective Tom Grant, and this is Detective Brad Logan. I want to thank you for coming in today."

"Thank me right, you made it real clear I had no choice but to walk here from my apartment today. This is harassment you know."

"Believe me we are not harassing you we just need to ask you some questions regarding the fentanyl you used that caused your overdose."

"Are you arresting me for using drugs because you have no evidence and the Safe Injection Site has no right to report me?" she remarked.

"We are not arresting you, this is simply a follow up interview," Brad replied, "We only want to ask you about the individual who provided the drugs, can you tell us his name and description?"

"Oh right, that would make me real popular out on the street for me to give you a dealer. I am not a snitch, so I can't help you."

"You realize this individual that gave you drugs nearly killed you," Tom interjected.

"But it didn't, and I am fine, so I am not getting involved in your search to arrest someone. I am careful and know what I am doing so this was a mistake pure and simple on my part. I won't let it happen again because I know how to take care of myself."

"Ms. Lester you are barely an adult and need to get help. Have you talked to rehabilitation counselors or is there a family member you can call?" Brad asked.

"I am adult enough and don't need anyone. Can I go or are you actually arresting me? I have seen it on TV that you either have to arrest me or let me go."

"You are free to go but I really believe you should consider getting help or the next time we may be filing a fatality report," Tom advised her.

Samantha just snorted and grabbed her jacket. She was escorted out of the station and back onto the street.

"Do you think we will see her again?" Brad asked.

"Quite possibly one way or another," Tom sighed.

Wednesday morning was cloudy, and it looked like it would rain as Tom drove into the station.

Tom drank his morning coffee thoughtfully as he went over notes and reports at his desk until Brad came in at 9:30 to collect Tom and travel to the apartment for the interview of Marion Casey.

On a hunch, Tom had downloaded to his phone the photo that surveillance had sent him of the two men who had met with Elliot Brown in Springbank Park.

They called up on the intercom and Mrs. Casey buzzed them in, meeting them at the apartment door.

"Marion is in the living room, but she is very nervous about this interview. She is very fragile over her slip back to drugs that happened on the weekend."

"Thank you, Mrs. Casey, we will be as considerate as possible in our discussion," Brad responded.

Tom and Brad followed Evelyn Casey into the living room of the apartment where Marion sat with her legs tugged under her on the sofa. Her look was tired, drawn, and pensive as they walked into the room. Her eyes darted up quickly and then returned to stare at her hands folded on her lap.

Tom observed that Marion was slight of built, her brown hair was neatly cut but when she looked up her brown eyes were sorrowful, and she appeared much older than her 39 years. It was saddening for Tom to contemplate what type of hell this lady had endured and what had led her to the place of using drugs in the first place.

"My name is Detective Tom Grant, and this is Detective Brad Logan from the London Police. We need to ask you some questions regarding the fentanyl that caused your overdose last weekend. We are not here to arrest you or harass you in any way. We just want to find out where this fentanyl is coming from to prevent others from being injured or killed."

"I will assist you if I can, but I am not sure I will be of much help," Marion responded.

"Can you tell us where you obtained the fentanyl and from whom last weekend?"

"I have been clean for months until last Friday, going to meetings and doing well. I met a man on Friday afternoon in the Tim Hortons in Byron when I went in for a coffee. I had heard that there were two guys that sold drugs outside that location.

"I wasn't really looking to buy but I got talking to this man, and he offered me the fentanyl as a gift. I don't know why I took it, but I did.

"I struggled when I got home Friday night with whether I should take it or get rid of it, but I gave in and injected the fentanyl. You are aware of what happened after that, thankfully my mom had checked on me and called emergency services."

"I can only imagine what you go through, can I ask you why you started to use drugs?" Tom questioned softly.

"It all started seven years ago when I was in a vehicle accident and ended up with severe chronic pain. My doctor prescribed oxycodone as a pain medication to ease the suffering. That worked for a while, but I needed more and more to remove the pain and the feeling of euphoria was addictive. I started taking higher doses to get that sensation. My doctor then said he was stopping the oxy, so he refused to write me prescriptions and the pain came back. I felt sick all the time, so I started buying pain pills on the street to ease my sickness plus I wanted to feel good again. I told my doctor about the problems, but he told me that I just needed to accept the pain and the fact the withdrawals from the oxy would subside and go away with time. I couldn't do that, so I stopped seeing the doctor and just bought my opioids wherever I could.

"A year ago, I came to the realization that I couldn't go on like this and I attempted suicide. After my hospitalization, my mother talked me into going into a rehabilitation program, then I joined Narcotics Anonymous and I have been clean until last weekend."

"What happened last Friday?" Tom asked.

"I was having a really bad week with pain and feeling low. I should have called my sponsor Friday but instead I went to the Tim Hortons, not really looking to score opioids but it was probably in the back of my mind. When he offered me the free dose, I gave in and took it. I made a mess of things."

Marion turned to her mother and started to cry, "I am truly sorry Mom, I have put you through so much and I just can't seem to get straight."

Evelyn Casey came over to sit beside her daughter on the sofa and held her sobbing shoulders, "I am your mother and I will always be here for you no matter what. We will get through this the same as we have gotten through everything else, I love you."

Tom and Brad sat quietly waiting until both mother and daughter had regained their composure.

"I really hope that things will work out for you and that you can find the strength you need," Tom said, "Get connected with professional help and stay in close contact with your NA sponsor and meetings. I understand that those can be a blessing and a real-life saver. Can we talk about the gentlemen who gave you the fentanyl last Friday, do you have his name, or can you describe him?"

"I only got his first name which was Pete, he was a larger man in his early thirties, his grey hair was in a brush cut and he had a mustache, I believe his eyes were brown.

"He weighed around 90 kilograms and his height was around 1.8 meters. He wore blue jeans and a blue T-shirt and a jacket. I remember noticing that he had a tattoo on his forearm, but I could only see the bottom that looked like a snake's tail."

Something in the description jogged Tom's thinking. He pulled out his cell phone and opened the picture that was sent from the surveillance detail on Elliot Carson.

"Do you recognize any of these men?"

"The larger man is the one we are talking about, Pete. The other is his partner but I don't know his name."

"Thank you Marion and Mrs. Casey, you have been a great help in providing us information we can act on and stop others from being potentially hurt or killed," Tom concluded.

Evelyn Casey walked the detectives to the apartment door.

"Thanks again Mrs. Casey."

"Take care of her," Brad added.

As they walked to the car, the two detectives discussed the fact that they now had a positive identification on one of the individuals involved in distributing the fentanyl on the weekend and also a definitive connection to Elliot Brown, their main suspect in the Shepherd's homicide.

They discussed the need to locate the two in the photograph regarding the drugs and see how and if they could find a more conclusive probable cause that could get them a search warrant for Elliot Brown's property.

Brad took on the task of getting more information on the man identified only as Pete and the mystery suspect. He had the photograph circulated and requested all uniformed officers to be on the lookout for the two men in the photo wanted as persons of interest regarding suspicious activity shown with Elliot Brown. The officers were also advised to detain the two for questioning.

Brad had arranged another interview for just after lunch at 1:30 with Carrie Anderson, the walker who had found and reported the body of Tom Sanders. Ms. Anderson had agreed to stop into the station and answer some follow up questions for the detectives.

At 1:30 p.m., Carrie Anderson arrived at the police station and asked for Detective Brad Logan. She was taken to the interview room and Tom and Brad joined her there.

"Good afternoon Ms. Anderson, I want to thank you for taking the time to come down and answer some follow up questions regarding the body of Mr. Sanders that you located on Saturday last," Brad started the conversation.

"Not a problem," she replied, "How can I help you?"

"We noted from the police report that the victim, Mr. Sanders, was a resident in the same apartment building where you reside. We wondered if you could provide any additional observations about him or anyone he might be associated with."

"I really did not know him well. I would run into him at the apartment mailbox or in the front lobby coming or going. I have never been in his apartment and have not seen him with anyone that I can remember from past meetings."

"Can you tell us if there have been any suspicious characters or individuals that you may have noticed coming or going in the building or in the vicinity in the past few weeks?"

"Nothing sticks out to me."

"One final request, can you go over the events of the date in question when you found Mr. Sanders body in the park."

"As I told the officers, I had crossed Commissioners Road heading into Springbank Park to go for a walk. I generally walk in the park on the pathways and trails when the weather is nice. That day I crossed into the park and walked along the pathway towards the washrooms and the parking lot at the west entrance to the park. Just past the washrooms, I cut through the tree lined grassed area to go down the hill towards the Thames River pathways. I noticed Mr. Sanders seated on the ground, leaning up against a tree trunk. He wasn't moving so I though he may be sleeping, but the way he was slumped over to the side concerned me. I went over to say good morning and check if he was alright, and that was when I found he was not responding to me. I tried to awaken him but when I couldn't I called 911 to provide assistance.

"The 911 officer asked me to remain there by the pathway and direct the emergency response to where Mr. Sanders was located, which I did.

"The emergency responders and the police officer arrived and eventually Mr. Sanders was removed on a stretcher. The police officer at the time questioned me and took down my statement."

"Did you happen to notice anyone else in the park or in the area where you found Mr. Sanders body?" Brad asked.

"There were some other walkers on the pathway and I was passed by a couple of bicycle riders but that is normal on the bike and walk paths in the park. No one was in the area where I found Mr. Sanders that I noticed."

"I want to thank you for your assistance Ms. Anderson and in the event that you remember anything out of line or unusual please give us a call, here is my card," Tom concluded the interview.

After Ms. Anderson had left, Tom and Brad regrouped again, still outstanding was the need to find and interview the final two individuals involved in Saturday's incidents, Bridgett Collins and Allan Jones. Both were listed as no home address, so they were counting on the uniformed officers to locate them and bring them to the station for questioning.

It was now four days since the rash of overdose cases on Friday evening and Saturday morning. No new cases had developed, which meant the word had gotten out on the street regarding the fentanyl in question or the dealers had modified the product to be less strong.

Tom spent the balance of the afternoon preparing himself for the ward councilors meeting to be held that evening going home relatively early to have supper and get changed for the 7:00 p.m. start time.

He arrived at the Civic Gardens Center at 6:35 p.m. It felt a bit strange to be here as he considered everything that had occurred in the past weeks.

The home of the Shepherds was located just a few blocks up on Jarvis Street off Springbank Drive. The body of Tom Sanders had been found in the park, a short walking distance from the Civic Gardens towards the far end of the park. The meetings between Mr. Brown, Pete someone and the other unidentified individual had occurred in the park. The fentanyl that had been given to Marion Casey had occurred down the street in Byron, and the diary of Debbie Shepherd had been located in a tree trunk in the park. This vicinity was becoming cross-linked between the fentanyl overdose case and the Shepherd's homicide without anything that could be directly tied together to connect them.

Tom entered the front doors of the Civic Center and proceeded to the right of the front entrance where a meeting room had been set up with chairs, a podium, a projector, and screen.

The ward councilor's assistant met him and introduced herself. She explained that the meeting would be opened by the city councilor who would explain general items arising from recent council meetings. She would then turn it over to the representative from the Middlesex London Health Unit to present on the opioid crisis in London and Middlesex County and the Overdose Prevention Safe Injection Site. Tom would then be asked to provide an update on the overdose incidents over the weekend and the investigation since the councilor had received numerous calls from area constituents as the park falls in her ward riding.

Tom took a seat near the front of the room and waited for the meeting to begin. Residents were arriving and coming into the seating area with coffee cups, some carrying notepads and pens. From a general standpoint, Tom could not identify if any were reporters who may be here at the ward meeting, but he was sure there would be at least one. He was relieved that there were no television news present, as he hated how he appeared on the TV newscasts. No matter how hard he tried, he always ended up looking like he was upset or foolish depending on the situation. "If I had wanted to be the 'face' of the department, I would have gone into the Public Relations Media Office not major crimes," he had commented in the past when the experiences had not gone very well.

Councilor Helen Campo came to the podium and did a sound check to ensure everything was working before she opened the meeting by welcoming everyone.

"We have a full agenda for the 90 minutes we have scheduled this evening, so I would like to get right into it.

"First I want to thank the representatives from the London and Middlesex Health Unit and the London Police Force for their willingness to come this evening and talk to us about the opioid crisis in our city. As we are well aware after this past weekend's occurrences, the presence of drugs is not confined to the downtown or less desirable sections of the city, we have had issues right here in ward 10.

"To start, I would like to spend a few moments updating everyone on the key topics that City Council has been working on over the past month. The ongoing work on the London Rapid Transit Plan continues with the decision for the engineering department to proceed on the environmental study based on the time line that has been tentatively set by council.

"I realize that this has been a long and sometimes bitter debate and has become one of the main topics of policy discussions for the candidates that are running in the municipal elections scheduled for next month. Our current mayor supported the proposal but with his decision not to stand for re-election the mayoral candidates are all being vocal on their views on the project.

"Everyone agrees that there needs to be something done about London's public busing system and the desire to access the federal transportation funds that have been tentatively allocated to London.

"In addition, the controversy over the amount of road infrastructure improvements that are ongoing throughout the city has caused concern for residents but will result in fixing a number of issues with the roads. 2018 has seen a significant number of projects being undertaken, some of which are very large and time consuming. We at council appreciate your patience and understanding through this roadwork season.

"Finally, the debate surrounding protected, safe bike lanes on many of our downtown streets is one that we, at council are trying to address and will continue to receive input on designs for specific streets and how this will tie into the rapid transit debate.

"Are there any questions on these or other topics that council is working on before we move to the main topic for tonight's meeting?"

Tom glanced around the room and noticed that approximately 30 people had gathered for the meeting, not sure how this number reflected against other ward meetings regarding whether it was a good or poor turnout.

One lady stood up, "My name is Sarah Gleason and I live on a side street off Boler Avenue where we have had a problem with a large pot hole in the road for months. I have complained to the city roads department and they came out early this summer and put loose gravel in the pot hole, but no one ever came back to fix it. The gravel has deteriorated, and the hole is large enough to pose a hazard to drivers in the area."

"Thank you, Ms. Gleason," the counselor replied, "My assistant will get your name and the location of the pot hole. City road works has been trying hard to catch up and get ahead of the pot hole issues that develop and my assistant will follow up."

The next gentleman who stood up wanted to discuss the issue with drivers who were going through the school zone in his neighborhood at excessive speeds. He stated that most drivers were not slowing down or obeying the flashing school speed zone signs.

The councilor again asked him to provide his name to her assistant and she would approach by law enforcement for follow up. There may be a need for the city to install speed bumps or traffic calming devices in the area of the speed zone. She would respond back.

The councilor then commented that since time was progressing she wanted to turn the meeting over to the representative from the London and Middlesex Health Unit to present on the opioid crisis in the city, but she would be staying after the meeting if there were any others who wished to talk to her and her assistant about individual issues in their areas.

She then introduced Margaret Spencer from the Middlesex London Health Unit.

Ms. Spencer turned on her power point presentation and proceeded to the podium.

"Good evening, thank you for coming this evening so that we can discuss the serious issue of opioid use in Middlesex London and what we, at the health unit are doing to try and help alleviate the problem of addiction and deaths.

"As you are all aware, the city suffered one of the worst weekends in our history last weekend regarding the number of deaths related to opioid overdoses, and I understand that Detective Grant will discuss the investigation into that later this evening.

"To begin, I want to give you some background information on the scope of the problem.

"Death rates have been fluctuating in Middlesex-London since 2005. The highest rate of deaths related to opioid toxicity was seen in 2012. In Ontario, the death rate has been slowly increasing. In 2012, our death rate was nearly nine per 10,000 population. Based on the 2011 census, the population was just under 475,000. This means we had over 40 deaths from opioid during that year.

"In 2013 and 2014, we saw a significant reduction in opioid related deaths but the rate in 2015 and 2016 has climbed.

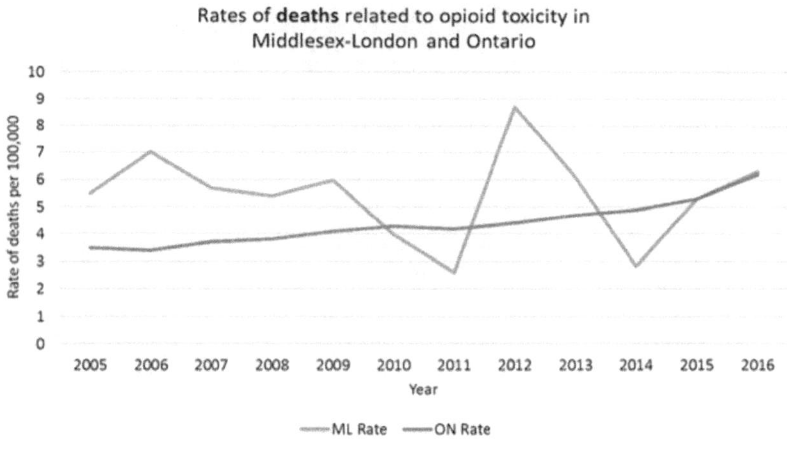

18

Note: Death rates for 2016 should be considered as preliminary and is subject to change

"In 2017 and 2018, the Health Unit has taken a significant step to enhance our services for prevention of deaths through the opening of the first Overdose Prevention Site to allow for safe injection use of drugs.

---

18 Data Source: Ontario Opioid-Related Death database, Office of the Chief Coroner for Ontario for the slides in the presentation. Accessible on the Public Health Ontario Interactive Opioid Tool

"In addition, there has been a steady expansion of the distribution of free naloxone kits that began in June 2014 under the Naloxone Program supported by the Ontario Ministry of Health and Long-Term Care. The program is a collaborative effort between the Middlesex-London Health Unit, Regional HIV/AIDS Connection, London Area Network of Substance Users and the London Inter Community Health Care.

"Even with the expanded intervention we have still seen a need to find more ways that we can further address the opioid crisis in Middlesex London.

"The goals of these changes has been to provide safe clean needles to reduce the transferal of disease in the population, allow for monitoring of the condition of the clients of the safe injection site to reduce overdose deaths and responses, to reduce the number of discarded used needles that are a problem throughout the city, and also to be a safe place for counseling and assistance with rehabilitation opportunities.

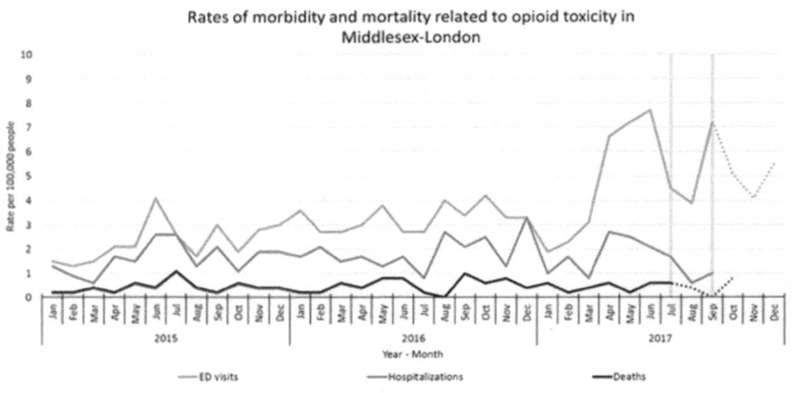

NOTE: Death data source changes after 2017-07 and Emergency Room visits (ED) data after 2017-09. Death data for 2016/17 is preliminary and subject to change.

"One of the main means of preventing opioid overdose deaths has been the number of naloxone kits that have been distributed in Middlesex-London that has steadily increased from its inception in June of 2014. It has leveled off at more than 500 kits distributed in each quarter in 2018 and the number of people reporting that they have administered a kit continues to increase.

"Naloxone is a medication used to block the effects of opioids, especially in the case of an overdose. When given intravenously, it works within two minutes and when injected into a muscle it works within five minutes; it may also be sprayed into the nose.

"The effects of naloxone last about half an hour to an hour so multiple doses may be required as the duration of action of most opioids is greater than that of naloxone.

"Also, the administration to opioid-dependent individuals may cause symptoms of opioid withdrawal including restlessness, agitation, nausea, vomiting, sweating, and fast heart rate.

"That is why emergency responders need to be called and the patient transported to a hospital for continued treatment of the overdose.

"The kits are supplied through local pharmacies or community organizations. The link to the list is located on the Ontario government web page at:

www.ontario.ca/page/naloxone-kits-free.

"The kits are free to a current opioid user or a past user who is at risk of using again, a family member, friend or other person able to help someone at risk of an opioid overdose, a client of a needle syringe program or hepatitis C program, an individual newly released from a correctional facility.

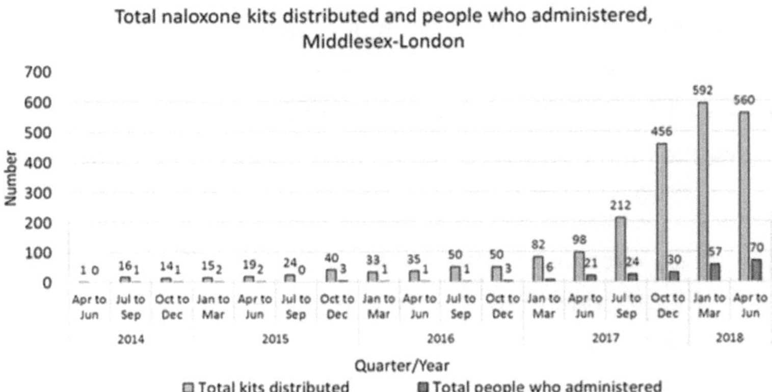

"Opioid related hospitalizations have been increasing generally over time in both Middlesex-London and Ontario. In recent years, the rate in Middlesex-London has been increasing at a higher pace then the province.

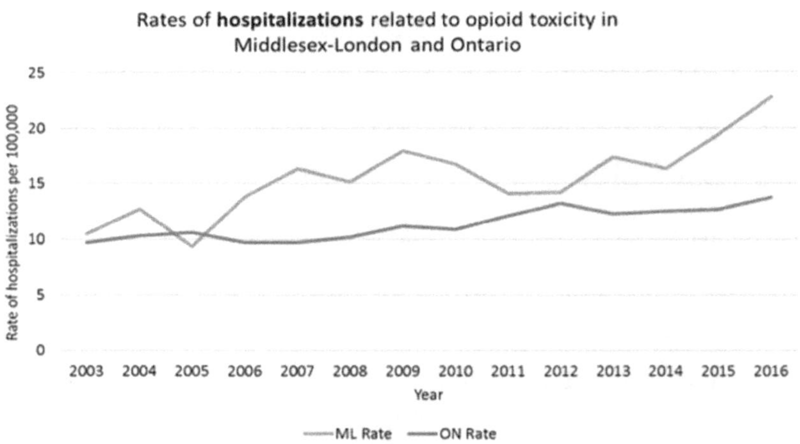

"We have an opioid crisis working group which includes representatives from the city of London, Middlesex-London Health Unit, regional HIV AIDS Connection (RHAC), London Inter Community Health Centre (LINC), Addiction Services of Thames Valley, London Police Service, London CAReS,

Southwest LHIN, London Health Sciences Centre (LHSC), EMS, as well as an indigenous community leader, and a person with lived experience.

"The work of the Opioid Crisis Working Group is currently focused on guiding the public consultation process related to Supervised Consumption Facilities in Middlesex-London.

"In conclusion some of the other strategies that the Middlesex-London Health Unit is coordinating are,

"The 'Street Nursing' outreach team that participates in locating, engaging, educating, and ultimately linking people to care, treatment, and basic needs programs. The end goal is to help decrease the spread of disease and support clients through their continuum of care in an environment where clients feel supported enough to reach their treatment goals.

"The needle syringe program is a community collaboration that provides a variety of services to clients including distribution of new injection and safer inhalation equipment, disposal of used equipment, naloxone and training to help prevent overdoses, education and information about safe injection or inhalation practices and referrals to support agencies and organizations in the community.

"In regard to the needle recovery program each year in London more than three million clean needles are distributed to people who inject drugs; of these, about 60% are recovered.

"If the public finds needles on public property, they can call 519-661-2489 ext. 4965 24 hours a day, seven days per week.

"The information I have presented plus additional information can be found at www.healthunit.com/opioids-middlesex-london-response which was modified June of this year.

"Are there any questions before I turn the podium over to Detective Grant?"

Tom noticed a couple who had been seated on the other side of the room rise to their feet. He had noticed that the gentleman had sat with his arms crossed in a posture that indicated he was not in agreement with the presentation.

"My name is Hillary," the lady started, "I live near Byron View Park and Whisper Wood Park that are located on Colonel Talbot Road. I have seen and heard individuals partying late at night in the parks, there are discarded needles everywhere. When I call the police, they will eventually come but there is never anything they can do to stop this from happening on a continuous basis. I am afraid to go there to walk my dog or take my children to the park. What is the city doing to put a stop to this?"

The ward councilor joined in, "If we have these problems please contact my office and we will follow up with the police department to try and get a better handle on it."

"That's not the point," the gentleman interjected. "I would like Ms. Spencer from the health unit to answer what all these 'programs' that are spending my tax dollars are doing to stop the problem."

Ms. Spencer replied, "The programs are doing a lot to significantly reduce the number of deaths related to drug use and to also cut down drastically on the number of used needles being discarded in public areas."

"What do these 'thousands' of naloxone kits cost us per year?"

"The kits cost approximately $60 each but when we consider that cost against the lives involved it is really negligible."

"Well I am opposed to this whole program," he continued, "If we stop coddling these people and just let them overdose and die, it will get rid of the problem through natural selection. In addition, the police need to do their job and get these people off the street and locked up. That may sound harsh, but I have a sister who waited for months for surgery that she needed because of the lack of funding for health care and we are wasting all this money on individuals who have no purpose or desire to better themselves in my opinion."

The couple then sat down, and Tom looked around the room, he noted many individuals who were clearly not in agreement with the couple based on their facial expressions, but he also noticed that a group of five or six individuals who had come in with the couple and their body language showed they were in agreement with the statement.

It was clear that they had attended the meeting with a sole purpose in mind, and Tom felt compassion for the Health Unit representative since there was no logical argument that you could make to these individuals.

He wondered what would develop in response to his presentation.

Ms. Spencer tried to respond diplomatically, "I can sympathize with the issues related to the funding of our health care system and the stress that can cause for individuals who are waiting for surgery but we cannot, as a society, turn our backs on those people who are trapped in the cycle of drug abuse. Drug abuse is a disease just like any other disease and we need to treat individuals who are suffering from that disease."

Councilor Campo then thanked Ms. Spencer and stated that Ms. Spencer would be available after the meeting if anyone wished to talk to her individually about the Health Unit programs.

"I would now like to introduce Detective Tom Grant of the London Police Services. Detective Grant is the lead investigator regarding the four overdose deaths that occurred in London this past weekend. Detective Grant."

Tom stood up and moved to the podium.

"Good evening, my comments will be short as we are nearly out of time.

"The London Police Services is currently investigating the fatalities of four people and the treatment of four other overdose victims this past weekend due to a strong lethal strain of fentanyl laced heroin that surfaced in London.

"The London Health Unit and its partner organizations did a fantastic job of getting the word out onto the streets on Saturday afternoon which we believe, went a long way towards stopping the rash of overdoses. We have not had any reports since then related to the fentanyl in question.

"The four fatalities all involved homeless individuals who were discovered too late to provide emergency support. The four that survived were fortunate that they had others with them either in their homes, at the safe injection site, or had companions on the street so that naloxone could be administered, and emergency services contacted for hospital follow up.

"The London Police Services has a lead on a suspect who we believe is the dealer or one of the dealers involved and we will be releasing more information when the investigation is complete.

"We appreciate the cooperation of the public in this investigation and other drug related cases and the Police Services applauds the work of the Middlesex-London Health Unit in its efforts to aid individuals and reduce the drug use concerns for our city.

"That is all the information we have at this time unless there are any questions."

Tom paused for questions but there were none, so he thanked everyone for coming and stated he would be available after the meeting if anyone wished to speak to him individually.

Councilor Campo then closed the meeting.

Tom observed the meeting attendees as they stood up and broke into two distinct groups, those who gathered with the couple and those who talked in smaller gatherings with many leaving quickly after the meeting.

Tom asked himself how we as a society could get to the point that individual lives mattered so little to so many.

One individual came up to Tom and wanted to talk.

He shared about his nephew who had died from an opioid overdose the past winter. He talked about the boys struggles as a teen and how he had become addicted. The police had arrested his nephew years ago for marijuana in his possession where the quantity classified him as possession with the intent to sell. He had gone to prison for a few months. He knew this was not the fault of the police and he didn't blame the police. Because of his criminal record, the boy could not get a steady job and his self-respect had declined ending in the night he overdosed on opioids.

The uncle had tried to help by petitioning the courts to expunge the young man's record and to get him into rehabilitation, but he had not been able to do anything to help. He was bitter about the legal system and wanted to know how these things could be allowed to happen. Now that marijuana was becoming legal next month and would not be a criminal offence, it just didn't seem fair and was such a waste.

Tom expressed his understanding for the gentleman's pain but had no real answer to provide, as all Tom could do was listen.

After the attendees dispersed, Tom excused himself to Councilor Campo and thanked Ms. Spencer for her presentation.

He drove home still concerned about the attitudes of some he witnessed this evening and the words shared by the uncle. He was now more convinced than ever that this may be the area he needed to focus on when his retirement was finalized: to become involved and try and help those who were working towards finding ways to help individuals.

After 46 years of marriage, Ann had quickly sensed Tom's mood when he arrived home at 9:00 p.m., and they had talked about the ward meeting and how Tom was feeling and what he was thinking about doing once he retired officially November 2nd, just four weeks from this Friday.

This was the first time the two of them had honestly spent time discussing the reality of Tom not being a police officer and how that would impact their lives. Putting all the joking aside, Ann asked Tom what he actually planned to be involved in after retirement because she knew he could not just be a sit at home retiree, he needed to be involved.

"In the back of my mind, I have been thinking about how I can get involved in social organizations, and I think that trying to help people caught up in this cycle of drugs and hopelessness is what I want to do. I would like to try and help young people who are lonely and hurting. To use my experience and my beliefs to engage positively through community and government agencies and through our church.

"When I meet some of these people I realize that, except for a stroke of fate, something different that happened in their lives, our sons could have ended up like those individuals who are lost instead of where they are. Something you have no control over as simple as who your parents are and how your life develops, or what happens to you as you are growing up can steer your life journey.

"Looking at the teenage girl Debbie Shepherd, good home, loving parents yet circumstances at school with other kids had cut down her self-worth by bullying her and taunting her dictating the path her life was taking.

"There is just too much nastiness out there today and someone or something needs to get involved to try and change that."

"I have always been proud of you and what you do," Ann commented, "but never more than when I listen to you want to save the world. You know people will say that it's impossible to save the world, but I remember the story of the star fish on the beach."

One day, an old man was walking along a beach that was littered with thousands of starfish that had been washed ashore by the high tide. As he walked, he came upon a young boy who was eagerly throwing the starfish back into the ocean, one by one.

Puzzled, the man looked at the boy and asked what he was doing. Without looking up from his task, the boy simply replied, "I'm saving these starfish, Sir."

The old man chuckled aloud, "Son, there are thousands of starfish and only one of you. What difference can you make?"

The boy picked up a starfish, gently tossed it into the ocean, and turning to the man said, "I made a difference to that one!"[19]

Thursday morning was cold and cloudy. The night had seen the temperature drop down to zero degrees Celsius leaving a white layer of frost over the grass and plants. Early October could be really nice weather, or it could bring snow, Tom had seen both, but this year looked like it would be a cold but clear Thanksgiving weekend.

Tom arrived at the station and, following his usual routine, got his morning coffee and went to his desk.

At 10:00 a.m., he got a call from Brad, the uniformed officers had located Bridgett Collins, one of the two homeless overdose victims from the past weekend this morning in Victoria Park.

They were bringing her into the station for an interview.

Tom and Brad came to the interview room and reviewed notes as they waited for Ms. Collins.

The door opened and a lady in her late twenties, early thirties entered the room.

"Good morning, I am Detective Tom Grant, and this is Detective Brad Logan, can we get you a cup of coffee or water?"

"Coffee would be good, two milks, three sugars," Bridgett answered.

---

19 **Adapted from The Star Thrower** (or 'starfish story') is part of a 16-page essay of the same name by Loren Eiseley (1907–1977), published in 1969 in The Unexpected Universe. **The Star Thrower** is also the title of a 1978 anthology of Eiseley's works (including the essay), which he completed shortly before his death.

Brad left the interview room to get the coffee, and Tom assessed Bridgett's physical appearance. She had dark black hair and green eyes but the wear and tear associated with the life of drug use showed in her face and in her posture. She had an overall appearance of defeat that left Tom wondering about the journey she had been through so far.

When Brad returned, they started the interview.

"We want to get some background information on the fentanyl that you used last Friday and where you obtained it."

"I got it from a friend, she had bought it from someone in Victoria Park and had enough for both of us. She had to go to social services before they closed and did not want to take the chance of being caught holding drugs. She asked me to keep it till later that evening.

"We were to meet up at 10:30 in the park. I waited but she hadn't come so just before 11, I decided to go ahead and shoot up without her. The fentanyl hit me real hard and I remember getting sleepy and confused very quickly. I heard one of my friend's voice, but I was not able to talk. I remember vaguely him making a phone call before I passed out and woke up with emergency response around me. They then took me to the hospital."

"Can you tell us who your friend is who obtained the drugs?"

"No, I am not going to get him involved, he didn't do anything except probably save my life. He's a friend."

"We just want to find out who was selling this fentanyl, it killed four people last weekend."

"Sorry but I can't help you with that. I didn't buy it, don't know who was selling it and I am not going to rat out my friend."

"Can you provide us with any help?" Tom asked.

"I can tell you that there have been a couple of new guys that have been around over the past few months and they have had a constant supply. Don't know their full names but one guy is big and goes by Pete, the other is a smaller guy and I heard others call him by the name of Smitty. Don't know if they are involved."

"Can you tell us anything else about these two individuals?"

"One thing I remember is that the way to recognize Pete is that he has a snake tattoo that runs from his shoulder down to his forearm. They say he can get really ugly if you don't pay up quick."

Tom thanked Bridgett for her help and called the uniformed officer to give her a ride back to Victoria Park.

"We need to find these two," Tom stated.

"Uniforms have their picture and are watching for them, but they haven't surfaced yet," Brad replied.

"Tell the uniformed officers if they locate them not to pick them up just yet but to advise the vice team, hopefully we can catch them in the act of selling rather than simple possession with intent. Make a more airtight case.

"In the meantime, we need to get identities on them and figure out how to connect them with our person of concern Mr. Brown. If we can connect them that would give us enough probable cause to dig deeper into Mr. Brown and obtain a search warrant for his home."

At 2:30 that afternoon, they got a call that uniformed officers had located the last victim from Saturday morning, Allan Jones and he was in the interview room in the station.

Again, Tom and Brad went to the interview room and sat across from a gentleman in his mid-forties, shoulder length black hair, and brown eyes.

"Good afternoon Mr. Jones, my name is Detective Tom Grant, and this is Detective Brad Logan. We would like to ask you some questions regarding the fentanyl you took last Saturday morning and where you obtained it."

"Okay," he replied.

"Can we get you a coffee or water?"

"Coffee would be nice, black."

Brad left the interview room returning with a cup of black coffee.

"Can you tell us where you are currently living?"

"Nowhere really, I have been spending some nights in the Mission Center shelter downtown but that is not the best place, other than that I have managed to couch surf at different apartments with people I know."

"Can you expand on what you mean regarding the Mission Center shelter?" Tom asked.

"Well the staff are great, and the Salvation Army tries their best but you have no real privacy and most of the time the other residents are simply trying to steal your stuff. You have to sleep with one eye open if you get my drift or else you will wake up with nothing. They do provide a warm cot and a good meal though, so I go there when I have to."

"Don't you have any family?" Brad asked.

"My daughter lives here in London with her husband. That's why I moved here from Toronto nearly a year ago. I stayed at their place for a few weeks when we first reconnected but she wasn't very comfortable with me being there and her husband told me to get out and not contact them again.

"I can't really blame her as I was not much of a father when she was growing up. I didn't provide well so her mother had to raise her mostly on her own because I would disappear for long periods. I have been a drug user all my life."

"In regards to last Saturday morning when you used fentanyl at the safe injection site can you tell us where you obtained the drug?" Tom queried.

"Sure, those guys killed people and nearly killed the rest of us with that poison. I don't snitch on dealers for obvious reasons, as I need to have a supply but those two have been nothing but trouble since they came on the streets.

"The big guy's name with the snake tattoo is called Pete Caruthers and his little sidekick is called John Smith, goes by the nickname of Smitty. They deal a lot in the Victoria Park area. I understand they have an apartment downtown over one of the stores on King Street."

"Thank you, Mr. Jones. That is very helpful," Tom pulled out a printed copy of the photo surveillance had taken of Elliott Brown and his two companions in the park,

"Could you look at this photograph and tell me if you recognize the men in it."

"Don't know the one guy but the other two with him are Caruthers and Smitty."

"Can you positively identify each one by pointing them out?"

Allan then reached out and indicated on the photo the identities of Pete Carruthers and John Smith.

"One final request, if we have a statement typed up regarding your positive identification would you be willing to sign it?"

"Why not if the statement is just to identify the two of them in the photo."

"That's all we require, Mr. Jones, and I want to thank you again for your assistance. Once you have signed the statement a uniformed officer will take you back to where you wish to go. May I suggest that you consider getting some professional help?" Tom replied.

"Appreciate it but I am too old and past the point of help, I could use another coffee while I am waiting."

Tom and Brad left to prepare the statement and had the uniformed officer bring Mr. Jones a refill on his coffee.

"Sad," Brad commented. "But we now have a positive identification on the two individuals and the photo tying them to Brown may be enough for the search warrant. I will run a criminal check on the names of these two and get us some background."

At the end of the day, Tom left the station and headed home. Despite this morning's weekend forecast the weather had decided to turn nasty and rain was coming down heavily as he drove. For the first time he could remember Tom wondered where homeless individuals like Bridgett and Allan that he had met that day would hold up out of the storm.

He never really considered these things, since the homeless and street people were simply a faceless presence to everyone else that no one thought about as they went to their dry and comfortable homes. Out of sight – out of mind.

As Tom and Ann ate their supper, Ann commented that she had been thinking today about their discussion from the night before.

"With the boys gone and your retirement maybe we should consider downsizing and selling the house, move into something smaller."

Tom looked around the dining room of the four-bedroom home they had lived in for most of their married life. The boys had grown up in this house, gone to school, sports, church activities, and these walls reflected their lives.

"That's an interesting thought," he replied, "what brought that on."

"I have been thinking for a while now that it may be a good idea to move to something smaller and more manageable. The stairs to the basement and the bedrooms have been getting harder and harder on my hips and knees as time goes by."

Tom suddenly realized that it had been twenty years since Ann had hip replacement surgery on both of her hips and the complaints about joint pain had become more frequent. He hadn't paid the stairs a lot of serious attention, but he now considered the fact they were both getting older and developing more aches and pains.

"You know that might be a good idea, with the changes happening in our lives it may be the right time to look for something smaller on one floor. I saw an apartment recently in an apartment building on Springbank Drive that was a good size; great views, underground parking, and the elevator meant no stairs."

"Which apartment building?" Ann asked.

"It's on Springbank Drive near the corner of Commissioners Road and it is called Springbank on the Park as it overlooks Springbank Park."

"Something to think about," Ann replied. "Let's think about it and discuss it further."

Tom knew in his mind that Ann was right and that the discussion would inevitably conclude that it was time to move. He just wasn't sure where he really wanted to end up living.

Friday morning brought the end of this workweek. Tom considered the weekend activities. With the Thanksgiving holiday Monday, the family would all be gathering at their place for Thanksgiving dinner. He looked forward to seeing the grandkids as it had been three weeks since they were over at the house. The routine Sunday after church dinner had been skipped by Tom Jr. and the family for the past few weeks as he had been tied up at work with a major project.

Brad came into the office with the background reports on Pete Carruthers and John Smith.

"What have we got?" Tom queried.

Brad read the report findings out loud:

"Peter Caruthers, current address listed on King Street in London, no driver's license. He had recently been residing in Toronto until approximately five months ago when he relocated to London.

Criminal Record listed charges for break and enter and drug possession which had resulted in short periods of prison time. The report verified that he was suspected of selling drugs, but no definitive evidence could be found and the charges had not proceeded.

John Smith, known associate of Peter Carruthers, no current address. Prior address was also unknown.

Criminal record listed charges for break and enter, assault causing bodily harm, drug possession. He had recently served twelve months in the Toronto East Detention center in Scarborough for assault causing bodily harm. He was released four months ago after which he relocated to London."

Tom felt they were actually getting somewhere on the fentanyl case and hoped that it would help tie up the dead end on the Shepherd's homicide.

The vice officers were provided with the background reports and photo of Pete Carruthers and John Smith and asked for surveillance on the two with the hopes of catching them in the act of dealing drugs.

Tom spent the balance of the day working on files in his office.

As he worked, he stopped to consider the fact that four weeks from today he would be leaving this office and the force.

He thought back 25 years to when he was promoted into the major crimes' division.

As a rooky detective, he had been assigned to a senior detective to learn the procedures much as Brad was doing currently with him.

The first major case he worked on was a serial murder case that was occurring at Christmas that year. It had been a sensational investigation with intense media scrutiny. The press had duped the perpetrator as the 'Christmas Ornament Killer' because he had abducted young women, torturing them before he killed them, and then left his signature mark – a small glass Christmas tree ornament – stuck in the victim's mouth.

It was all hands-on deck, and it had taken four months and five homicides before the department was able to identify the perpetrator.

Tom returned to his computer, and he noticed that the police station was clearing out early with the upcoming long weekend.

Brad stopped into Tom's office and asked if there was anything Tom needed him to do before he ducked out for the weekend.

Tom said there was nothing that they could work on at this point and Brad advised that he was driving up to his parents place in Muskoka for the weekend but could be reached on his cell phone if he was needed.

Tom told him to have a good trip and stay safe, as the roads would be busy.

Shortly after Brad left Tom also decided to pack up for the long weekend and shut down his computer and office, heading home.

Over supper, Ann brought up the subject of selling and moving that they had discussed the prior evening.

"I thought about what you said, and I have been looking online at the apartments at Springbank on the Park on Springbank Drive. I have actually been looking at apartment listings for a few weeks now, so I called the rental agent and made an appointment to go over and see them tomorrow afternoon at 2:00 p.m. I also called a realtor and she is coming over here tomorrow at 10 a.m.to look at the house and give us some ideas on the sale value of our home."

"My goodness you didn't let any grass grow under your feet." Tom responded.

"If you don't want to, I can call and cancel."

"No, I agree it's time we look at our options. I can't live in the past or stay stuck in the present. I need to make plans for our new adventures together."

They continued to chat about what the future might hold, what it would be like when Tom is home all the time and how they were going to adjust.

First thing Saturday morning Tom made his pot of coffee in the kitchen while Ann moved about the house busily straightening beds and clearing away books, magazines, and other items that had been left out.

"You do realize that the realtor is only coming to tell us what the place is worth not to buy it or show it," Tom commented.

"It doesn't hurt to tidy up the place. We do have the family all coming over on Monday for Thanksgiving dinner and this gives me a head start."

The realtor from the Sutton Group realtors arrived at 10 a.m. sharp. She introduced herself and gave Ann her card.

"What are you looking to get for your home?" she asked.

"We have never had the house appraised since we bought it 25 years ago, so we have no real idea. I will trust you to advise us."

Ann then proceeded to give the realtor the guided tour of the home, and Tom remained in the kitchen drinking his coffee. He knew that his expertise was not of much value in this instance and he would rely on Ann to be the expert and answer any questions the realtor had.

"We have a strong sellers' market right now in London so I would estimate that this home would run in the three fifty to four hundred thousand range. I can go back to the office and run a pricing comparison with similar homes that have sold recently and give you a better idea if that works."

"That would be fine," Ann replied, "You can call me on my cell phone when you have it."

The realtor thanked them and said she would be back to them shortly.

Tom decided that they needed to go out for lunch and stop into the Farmers Market to pick up fresh vegetables for Monday to go with the traditional Turkey dinner.

They drove to the Farmers Market at the Western fairgrounds and walked around the stalls picking out vegetables and other produce. Ann also picked up bread and pastries from a bakery stall as well as some fresh homemade pumpkin pies from the Mennonite bakery stand for Monday's dinner.

Tony's Famous Italian Restaurant on Dundas Street had opened at 11 a.m. so they stopped there for lunch. Tom liked the upscale Italian food they served and the variety on the menu which came at reasonable prices.

After lunch, they took the purchases from the market home and then left to make their 2 o'clock appointment at Springbank on the Park.

Tom remembered the secure entry that allowed for controlled access into the building lobby and mentioned to Ann that he liked the security. It would be nice to be able to go away and travel if they wanted to without having to worry about the apartment.

They called the building rental agents cell phone and the agent buzzed them into the lobby advising that he would be down shortly to meet them.

Ann observed the lobby fireplace, couches, and the bubble water wall that Tom had described from his previous visit when he interviewed a witness in the building.

The agent arrived and introduced himself.

Ann had mentioned that they were interested in a two bedroom plus den unit, and he told them he could show them a model they had on the seventh floor overlooking the park.

They rode up the elevator and went to apartment 520. The apartment was facing the front of the building. It was furnished as a model, and they walked through viewing the granite tops in the kitchen, wood floors in the living room, dining room, and hallways. The apartment had two bedrooms, the master with an on-suite bathroom and walk in closet, and the second was also a good size with a second family bathroom in the hallway that had a tub. The den was smaller but cozy with frosted French glass doors.

Ann was enthralled by the view off the balcony overlooking high above Springbank Park. The apartment was listed as the fifth floor but due to the underground parking taking up the first two floors as P1 and P2 the fifth floor was in reality, seven stories and Ann could see above the trees all the way to the high-rise buildings in the north of London.

The agent then took them back to the first floor where the elevator opened in the rear to access an exercise room, pool, sauna, hot tub, and a games room. Outside the exercise room was a patio area with gas barbeques that were available for the residents to use at their leisure.

At parking level 2, the elevator opened to the underground parking from the rear of the elevator and allowed access to a library with couches and a fire place, as well as a theatre room that were designed to look out like a balcony over the front entrance lobby.

They then proceeded back to the rental agent's office and went over any questions and the details of the lease.

"We haven't actually put our house up for sale at this point so we can't commit to any lease." Tom remarked.

"That's not a problem," the agent stated, "We a have a number of residents who have retired and needed to sell their homes before moving in. We have an option that allows you to sign a future lease for three months from now so that you can sell your home. Based on the London real estate market that has not been an issue, and if you sell earlier you can advance the move in date or we can extend it based on the closing date of your homes sale."

"But how do we know you will have an apartment like the model available when we would be," Ann asked.

"If you like that unit we can sign the option specifying unit 502, and we will continue to use it as a model until you are ready to move in. We will just need two-week notice to take out the furniture, paint and touch up."

Ann looked at Tom, and he could see that she had fallen in love with the apartment.

"Can we come back Tuesday late afternoon and sign the option after we talk to our realtor to finalize the listing of our home." Tom asked.

"That will be fine, I will mark a complimentary hold on the unit until after Tuesday. Call me and we can arrange a time."

Tom and Ann left the apartment building and got in their car.

"What do you think?" Ann questioned, "I do like the apartment and the location. Could you be comfortable living in an apartment?"

Before Tom could answer Ann's cell phone rang.

It was the realtor, and she had done a comparison search on their home.

"I would recommend that you list the property at four hundred and twenty five thousand which will likely end up with a bidding war that could provide you an offer over list price."

"Let's do it," Tom remarked, "It's time to strike while the iron is hot."

The realtor asked if she could come back later this afternoon with the listing paperwork, and Ann told her that would be fine.

Since they were still in the parking lot of the apartment building, they called the rental agent back and said they had decided to sign the option on the apartment as they had just discussed their home sale with the realtor and were listing it today.

The apartment agent joined them back in the lobby, and they proceeded up to his office. As they went over the paperwork, Ann mentioned the only thing she really didn't like was the smaller fridge in the apartment as theirs is a French door with built in water dispenser. The agent made the suggestion that if they were open to signing a three-year lease the owner would upgrade the fridge to a French door unit with internal water as part of the deal. The rent would also be fixed for the three-year period.

Tom agreed and they wrote up the paperwork accordingly.

They left and went home to meet with the realtor and sign the listing agreement.

That evening they sat and reflected on the day and what had occurred. The real estate sign would go up Tuesday with the home being listed on the web site Wednesday morning. The realtor would have a photographer come over to take pictures late Tuesday afternoon to allow Ann time to 'stage' the rooms.

She had provided a guide on how to stage the rooms for the best first impression, but overall she had felt there really wasn't a lot of decluttering for them to do.

Tom commented to Ann that it would be an interesting Thanksgiving dinner on Monday with the family when they would break the news.

Sunday went as usual with church and visiting. The family was not coming over that day because of the big dinner on Monday with the exception of their son Kevin who was staying in residence at the university even though the university was in London.

The university wanted all first-year students to stay in residence regardless of where they lived.

Kevin always took the opportunity for his mom's homemade meals, and he was keeping up the Sunday tradition of joining them for church in the morning and coming over for lunch and dinner in the afternoon.

Tom and Ann did not broach the subject of their impending move, as they wanted to share it with the whole family on Monday.

142

CHAPTER FIVE:
WEEK FOUR

Monday October 8th, Thanksgiving Day was a cold, clear, and bright sunny fall day.

Kevin arrived at 10 a.m. and proceeded to lounge on the couch next to his dad.

Tom was watching the Canadian Broadcast Company (CBC) morning news which was doing a special report on the Canadian Thanksgiving.

"A lot of people think that the holiday is just a Canadian version of American Thanksgiving, but the Canadian celebration actually happened 40 years before the American pilgrims had their dinner. In 1878 the British explorer, and occasional pirate, Martin Frobisher held a feast of thanksgiving in Newfoundland. Frobisher was giving thanks that he and, well, most of his crew had come back from a rough trip through the Arctic looking for the Northwest Passage. After storms and cold and getting lost, Frobisher was sorry he hadn't found the Passage but very happy to be alive. This meal wasn't too tasty, coming out of ship's storage and tin cans but it started a tradition of being grateful for what food they had."

The announcer then went on to state that

"Thanksgiving has been officially celebrated annually in Canada since November 6, 1879 and the actual date varied each year, commonly the third Monday in October.

January 31, 1957 the Governor General of Canada, Vincent Massey issued a proclamation stating, 'A day of general thanksgiving to almighty God for the bountiful harvest with which Canada has been blessed – to be observed on the second Monday in October.'"

Kevin took the remote control and proceeded to look up what time the Canadian Football League Thanksgiving Day Classic was coming on that afternoon for the nationally televised doubleheader.

That was one tradition that Tom knew coincided with the American Thanksgiving, the holy grail of football.

Tom went into the kitchen to help Ann set up the table. Tom Jr. and the family were scheduled to arrive around one and the afternoon would consist of the boys in front of the television and him playing in the back yard with the grandkids. Ann and Gladys, Tom Jr.'s wife, would be hard at work in the kitchen getting the turkey, mashed potatoes, stuffing, etc. ready to eat at 4:00 p.m. sharp.

The afternoon went exactly as planned and the whole family sat down to eat at the dining room table.

"We have some news to share," Ann stated. "This is the last Thanksgiving that we will be gathering here for dinner."

The family looked confused and baffled.

"We have decided to sell the house and move into an apartment."

The room filled with questions and reminiscences about their home and everything that has happened here. Everyone agreed that it was a good idea but the nostalgia went on throughout the meal.

On Tuesday morning, Tom got to the office and saw that his office phone light was blinking a message. He picked up the phone and there were two message.

The first from Friday evening was a message from the lead officer on the Springbank Park surveillance team. It advised that Elliot Brown and the other two individuals in question had met in the park Friday afternoon. Surveillance had taken more photographs and in a couple they were able to capture the image of Elliot passing a brown paper bag package to the larger of the two men. The message advised that the photos had been sent to Tom's email.

The second voice message was from Vice Narcotics asking Tom to return their call as they had arrested Peter Carruthers and John Smith on Monday and the two men were in custody.

Tom called vice first and talked with the duty officer who advised that the arrest report would be sent by email to Tom's attention.

Tom opened the photographs from Friday afternoon's surveillance on Elliott Brown and observed the distinct capture of the transfer of the brown paper bag from Elliot to Peter Caruthers. He noted on the photo that there was a logo of a flying bird on the outside of the bag. The logo image was very specific and after a quick internet search, he concluded that it did not appear to be from any business or organization.

The vice departments detailed electronic arrest report arrived in Tom's inbox.

The officers had undertaken an operation on Monday afternoon in Victoria Park. The two individuals Peter Carruthers and John Smith had been approached by an undercover policewoman wanting to purchase opioids. After discussion, the gentlemen had agreed to sell the officer fentanyl. Once they had completed the transaction, the undercover officer, assisted by other undercover officers who were stationed in the park had seized and arrested the suspects. They found enough fentanyl in the perpetrators possession to charge both for trafficking.

The lead officer had obtained a search warrant for the apartment of Mr. Carruthers, and they had executed it with CID officers later Monday afternoon.

In the apartment, they had found weapons, cash, and a brown paper bag containing a supply of fentanyl in small individual plastic bags. The report noted that the brown paper bag had a logo of a flying bird on the outside.

In addition, the CID officers had located another brown paper bag in a dresser drawer that field tested positive as a potential match to the batch of fentanyl laced heroin mixture that had resulted in the overdose deaths under investigation. The sample was scheduled by CID for a lab analysis Tuesday morning to verify.

The Criminal Investigation Division (CID) processed the apartment for prints and dusted the paper bags. The individual plastic bags contained within the larger bags were also fingerprinted.

Tom called Brad and went over the morning revelations.

"I have asked that CID send me over a photo of the paper bag to compare it against the one in the surveillance photos of Elliot Brown. Hopefully if we get a match on the fingerprints to Brown we will be able to arrest him for the drug case. That will give us the basis for probable cause for the search warrant to search his premises."

"We will need to be very careful on the wording of the search warrant since we will be searching, based on the potential drug charges. We need to ensure we don't make any evidence we may find regarding the Shepherd case to be classed potentially as inadmissible."

"Should we interview Carruthers and Smith?" Brad questioned.

"Not at this time, we don't want them to spook Brown. At this point, we will let the narcotics team process the two of them on the trafficking charges, and if the fentanyl that was found in the apartment or the paper bag comes back as a positive lab match to the drugs that caused the rash of overdoses we will upgrade the trafficking charge with four counts of manslaughter depending on what the crown attorney advises.

"I am going to contact the crown attorney and fill him in on our investigation."

Tom called the crown attorney and arranged for him and Brad to stop into the crown attorney's office.

They laid out the case they were building against Elliot Brown, the connecting evidence that they had and how this all tied into their suspicions.

Tom discussed the fact that they needed more time to connect all the dots and make a concrete case before Elliot Brown was fully aware of what they were putting together, and this meant they needed to get a search warrant for his premises.

The crown agreed to request that the judge holdover the two prisoners based on eminent flight risk and past criminal record at their initial court appearance this afternoon.

The crown advised that this will only likely stick for 48 to 72 hours at most before their lawyer's petition and get a bail hearing.

Tom thanked the crown attorney and stated that should give them the time they needed before Elliott Brown gets wind of the police's knowledge of his implication in the drug case.

The two detectives were now on a fast track of activity over the afternoon.

The CID analysis of the fentanyl-laced heroin found in a drawer at Carruthers' apartment had been confirmed as a definite match to the drugs that had been involved in the overdose cases.

The flying bird logo on the brown paper bag was a match to the photograph of the logo on the bag that was handed by Elliot Brown to the two arrested on drug trafficking charges.

The paper bag with the bird logo and the individual plastic baggies containing the drugs inside had been dusted by CID for fingerprints and had provided positive matches to the two arrested individuals and Elliot Brown.

The packaging containing the fentanyl laced heroin had been handled so much that the fingerprints were smudged and degraded to the point they could not get a positive match too Elliot Brown.

The crown attorney called Tom after the initial hearing and advised that the judge had agreed to hold over the two suspects on the drug trafficking charges, but their legal aid attorneys had immediately filed for a joint bail hearing. The hearing was scheduled for the following Friday on the charge of drug trafficking.

Tom and Brad discussed strategy, and they realized they needed to get the crown attorney to increase the charges based on the evidence to include four counts of first or second-degree murder in order to provide leverage to pressure the pair in custody.

Under the Canada Criminal Code (*RSC 1985 c. C-46 first degree murder is defined and classified as first degree when it is planned and deliberate 231 (2).*

(7) all murder that is not first-degree murder is second degree murder.

The crown agreed to add the charges of second-degree murder based on the four overdose deaths related to the trafficking of the heroin-laced fentanyl but stated more information would be required to modify to first-degree murder.

The criminal code did have wording that could be used to change the charges to first degree murder under Section 231 (6.1) to claim the individual's actions fell under the heading of criminal organizations while committing an indictable offence under the Controlled Drugs and Substance Act (S.C. 1996, c, 19) – possession, sale, etc., for use in production or trafficking in substance.

231 (6.1) irrespective of whether a murder is planned and deliberate on the part of a person, murder is first degree murder when:

(b) the death is cause by that person while committing or attempting to commit an indictable offence under this or any other Act of Parliament for the benefit of, at the discretion of or in association with a criminal organization.

The crown attorney was agreeable to adding the second-degree murder charges based on the evidence as it stood but advised Tom and Brad that in all likelihood the charges would be reduced to four counts of manslaughter during plea-bargaining in addition to the trafficking charges.

The crown advised, "Manslaughter is defined under the statutes as a homicide committed without the intention to cause death, and the crown attorney believed it fell under the definition of: An unlawful act – when a person commits a crime that unintentionally results in the death of another person. For example, an individual punches someone in the face and the person dies of his or her injuries, or someone fires their gun carelessly in public and unintentionally shoots a bystander."

In this case the sale of the heroine laced fentanyl that resulted in the deaths of the four individuals.

Tom told the crown attorney that was workable as they wanted to use the murder charge as a means to get Pete Carruthers and John Smith to positively implicate Elliott Brown with the heroin laced fentanyl.

Everything was building towards Thursday morning's interrogation of Carruthers and Smith with the intent of bringing in Elliott Brown Thursday afternoon. Elliott would be included in the drug trafficking charges based on the results of the interviews and the fact they could definitely show the link with the surveillance photos, the paper bag flying bird logo and the presence of Elliott's fingerprints on the bag and drugs.

Brad asked, "What if Carruthers and Smith don't positively connect Brown to the heroin laced fentanyl?"

They discussed how they could potentially use the evidence of pattern to link Brown to the heroin-laced fentanyl based on him leaving his home with brown paper bags, meeting the two traffickers in the park and returning home without the paper bags.

Tom realized that this would be circumstantial at best which meant they really needed to have Carruthers and Smith implicate Brown but it could go one way or the other.

Tom felt that either way it should be enough to get a warrant to search Brown's home from the judge when they arrested him.

On Thursday morning, Tom and Brad drove to the Elgin-Middlesex Detention Centre located at 711 Exeter Road in London.

Pete Carruthers and John Smith were brought into two separate interview rooms, and Brad and Tom undertook the interviews one at a time.

The second-degree murder charges had been served on the two Wednesday afternoon and their public defenders had discussed the charges last night in private with their clients, so Tom and Brad knew they were aware of the new charges being placed.

The plan was to try and get details regarding the heroin-laced fentanyl and hopefully to get one or the other to give up Elliot Brown's connection as the master mind and supplier.

They knew Elliott had been cautious, not allowing himself to be the one out there in the public but having these two be the public face of the operation. He had been clever and had it not been for the Shepherd investigation there would have been no definite means to directly connect him to the drug operation.

Tom intended to use the threat of potentially raising the charges to first-degree murder as a means to try and up the stakes during the interviews.

The first interview was with the Pete Carruthers as he was the registered occupant on the apartment where the drugs were located based on his signature on the lease.

He was sitting with his arms crossed over his chest behind the interview table with his legal aid attorney and glared when Tom and Brad entered.

The detectives introduced themselves and stated they were here to interview Pete Carruthers regarding the details surrounding the trafficking charges and the second-degree murder charges related to the four individuals who had died from overdoses from the heroin laced fentanyl.

First off, Tom stated that the drug trafficking charges were a done issue as both Pete and John had sold fentanyl to an undercover police officer. The main issue they wanted to discuss was the drugs located during the search of Pete apartment which positively linked him to the four homicides that had occurred as a result of the trafficking of those drugs.

Our first question relates to where you got the supply of the drugs in question and who is the individual behind this operation.

"I never sold those drugs that killed those people," Pete exclaimed, "The murder charges against me are bogus."

"That's not the total truth in this instance as we have the sworn testimony of two of the overdose survivors that identifies you as the one selling the drugs in question based on a positive identification from a photograph and from the description of the snake tattoo on your forearm," Tom interjected.

Pete looked over at his attorney quickly.

"We are not aware of any statements against Mr. Carruthers from third parties at this time," Pete's lawyer stated.

"I am sure you will have those discussions with the crown attorney," Brad said, "But we are telling you that Pete here is linked definitively to the sale of the drug that caused the deaths in this case. That specific lethal drug mixture was also found in Pete's apartment, so we are convinced we have an undeniable link to all these charges."

Pete sat back in his chair and had a distinctly more worried look to his features. Turning to his lawyer, he blurted.

"You told me that possession and trafficking of the drugs was all they had and even if heroin cut fentanyl was found it could not prove that I am involved with the sale of those drugs and the deaths. You said everything for the second-degree murder charge was coincidental and you would not allow it to stand up in court!"

"Mr. Carruthers, I advise you to be quiet," The lawyer cut in, "This is a fishing expedition on the part of the detectives and you are only going to hurt your own case if you persist."

Carruthers sat back again in his chair and glared at the lawyer.

"What exactly are you asking my client?" he asked the detectives.

"We believe that Mr. Caruthers and Smith are simply the front face for someone else farther up the supply chain and we want the information on who that person is," Tom replied.

"I would like to converse with my client privately if you could give us a few minutes."

"Not a problem," Tom answered, "We are going to interview Mr. Smith and we will then come back to continue this discussion."

Tom and Brad closed their notebooks and headed out the door of the interview room. Brad glanced back and observed Pete and his lawyer huddled closely in obvious earnest discussion before he closed the door.

The pair of detectives now entered the interview room containing John Smith and his legal aid attorney.

Mr. Smith was much more nervous than his colleague Pete as they entered, leaning forward against the interview table and glancing furtively around the room.

The detectives again went through their introduction identical to the interview with Pete Caruthers.

Mr. Smith's lawyer started the discussion by stating, "That although John had been present and arrested as an alleged party to the trafficking charges for the sale of the drug to the undercover officer he had simply been in attendance at the time of the occurrence, an innocent by stander. He had not been aware of Mr. Carruthers intended action and was not involved with the drugs that were found in Pete Caruthers apartment or the sale of the heroin laced fentanyl to the four individuals who died due to their overdose.

His name is not on the lease and although he has associated with Mr. Caruthers he has no connection above the fact that he is an individual who was at the wrong place at the wrong time."

"Regarding the sale of the drugs to the officer, your client was not just a bystander but was an active participant in the sale with his partner regarding the trafficking charges. We have your client's fingerprints on the bag and drugs found in Mr. Caruthers apartment, and we also have surveillance footage of your client clearly receiving the package of drugs with the distinctive flying bird logo from a third individual earlier in the week before the arrest," Tom stated.

"I have not been made aware of any surveillance footage," The lawyer responded.

"That will all be provided to you by the crown attorney regarding the trafficking charges, our interest is whether your client can identify the third-party individual that provided the package and information regarding the heroin laced fentanyl that was found in Mr. Carruthers apartment?"

"As I stated, my client Mr. Smith is not a listed resident at Mr. Carruthers apartment and therefore has no connection to the heroine laced fentanyl found in those premises and therefore cannot be linked to any murders."

"That's interesting," Brad replied, "As Mr. Caruthers is claiming that the drugs in question belonged to your client and he was not aware that John had stashed them in his apartment."

Brad knew this was not a true statement but was allowable deception during the questioning of the suspect.

"Bull shit," John burst out. "Those drugs were Pete's and I don't have any idea who he sold any of them to."

"Actually, Mr. Smith we have sworn statement from survivors of the overdoses that occurred from the heroin laced fentanyl that have positively identified you as a co-trafficker with Mr. Caruthers in the sale of those drugs in question that caused the homicides," Tom replied.

"What questions exactly are you wanting my client to answer?" the attorney interjected.

"We want the name of the individual who is behind the drug trafficking ring and provided your client with the heroin laced fentanyl. The first of these two who provide us with the information is up for special consideration with the crown attorney." Brad replied, "Personally I believe that Pete Caruthers is the main actor in this pair and by giving up this information before he does your client may benefit."

"We are investigating the possibility of having the crown attorney amend the charges to first degree murder based on the indictable drug trafficking case if we find that your client was working as part of a criminal organization," Tom added.

John and his lawyer huddled together at the other side of the table but unlike Pete's attorney, they did not request privacy by asking the detectives to leave.

After several minutes of whispered discussions, the attorney faced the detectives.

"To be clear, if Mr. Smith cooperates in this regard then your department will be asking the crown for leniency in my client's case and is subject to a potential plea bargain, is that correct?"

"That's the agreement, if your client can provide the name and a sworn statement that implicates the third party in the provision of the drugs in question," Tom said.

"Agreed, John answer their questions."

"Pete and I moved here to London at the request of Elliot Brown. He told us he had a steady supply of heroin and fentanyl and wanted us to be the street front for the operation.

Elliot lives on Jarvis Street in the second house from the end of the dead-end street under the name of Elliot Carson. I have never been to his house. We would meet in Springbank Park across the street from where Elliott's street was, and Elliott would provide packages of the drugs to sell and then collect the proceeds from the sales that had happened.

"We were given a 10% cut of the sales prices that Elliott set but sometimes Pete would add on a few extra dollars as a 'service charge' that he didn't tell Elliott about."

"Can you tell us about the afternoon of Friday September 7th and the subsequent events that occurred on the Friday evening and following Saturday regarding the heroin laced fentanyl?" Tom asked.

"On the afternoon of Friday September 7th, we had met Elliott in the park as usual, and he had provided us with the brown paper bag of what he referred to as special fentanyl for us to sell.

"That weekend we had sold the drug to several individuals on the Friday evening and Saturday morning, even giving our first baggie to a lady outside the Tim Hortons in Byron. It was late Saturday morning when we heard on the street that people were overdosing and dying from the drugs. Pete contacted

Elliott and asked him what to do. Elliott said to stop selling it, and Pete stashed it in his apartment. The intent was to talk with Elliott and get directions the next time we met.

"When we met up the next week with Elliott he gave us a new parcel and he told us to bring back the other stuff next time we met, and he would reduce the dose of heroin in the fentanyl by mixing in small quantities with new batches of fentanyl to reduce the potency.

"We never got the chance to return the package before we were arrested, and you searched Pete's apartment.

"We never intended to kill anyone, we thought the stuff was the same regular heroin or fentanyl that we had got from Elliott before to sell."

"We want you to view a photo taken from a surveillance that occurred last Friday in Springbank Park and verify if the third person is Elliot Brown," Tom asked showing John the photo of the bag exchange.

"Ya that's Elliott," he responded.

"Thank you, Mr. Smith, I now need you and your lawyer to write up everything you have just told us even though we have it on tape from the camera here in the interview room so that we can be perfectly clear regarding your statement. We will advise the crown attorney of your cooperation including the sworn statement that you were not aware of the lethal consistency of the drug in question when you engaged in the trafficking. It will be up to the crown and your attorney to discuss how this will be taken into consideration regarding the current second-degree murder charges," Tom stated.

"I would like to discuss the details with the crown attorney as soon as possible before my client signs the statement," John's lawyer responded.

Tom and Brad left as the attorney and John started to write up his statement. They noted that the attorney was also on his cell phone which was likely to the crown attorney.

"How do you feel regarding the result of that interview?" Brad asked.

"Good, I think that Mr. Smith is a follower and he will be going away for a long spell for the trafficking and possibly the manslaughter charges. Pete and Elliott on the other hand are the ones I really want to get on the murder charges."

The detectives walked back into the interview room where Mr. Caruthers and his lawyer waited.

"My client is willing to answer your questions," the lawyer responded.

"Sorry to inform you but Mr. Smith has already cut his deal through his attorney and has given us Mr. Elliott Brown and the information on the whole operation," Tom stated

"Wait a minute," Pete interjected, "My lawyer told me we could cut a deal here, this is not fair that weasel Smith gets a deal and I don't! I am being railroaded!"

"You had the first opportunity when we were here to interview you first, but you wanted privacy with your attorney. Mr. Smith and his attorney were more cooperative and willing to come forward during the initial interview," Brad added.

"My client is willing to cooperate."

"Best I can do is to allow Mr. Caruthers to provide a statement and if it collaborates Mr. Smith we will advise the crown attorney of his action," Tom replied.

"What do you want to cover in the statement?"

"How Elliott Brown is involved as the main supplier and that Mr. Caruthers works for him in the distribution of the drugs. We need the details regarding the heroin-laced fentanyl and how it was supplied by Mr. Brown and if Mr.

Carruthers advised Mr. Brown about the deaths that it caused. We need Mr. Brown's reaction to that news."

"If my client does that you verify that you will advise the crown attorney that he did cooperate with the investigation?" asked the public defender.

"Yes. But I do have one other question for your client. On the afternoon of September 7th when your client met with Mr. Brown in the Park and transferred the package in question did he notice anyone else in the vicinity?"

"I remember there was a young girl who was in the park and she saw us, but Elliott said not to worry as she was just the neighbor's kid from next door to his house. He said she was a loner and wouldn't have seen anything of consequence," Pete responded.

Brad advised Caruthers and his lawyer that they needed them to include what Pete had just described in answering that question in his statement.

Tom and Brad left Pete and his attorney to write up his statement.

"We need to have Elliot Brown picked up and obtain a search warrant to search his house. I am becoming convinced that Elliott Brown saw Deborah Shepherd who observed them make the exchange in the park and that may be the motive that got her killed after Elliott learned about the overdose deaths," Tom mused.

They drove back to the station and contacted the crown attorney who said he would get the search warrant for tomorrow morning and issue a warrant for Mr. Brown's arrest.

On Friday morning when Tom arrived at the station, the crown attorney advised that the search and arrest warrants for Elliott Brown were in his office. Tom contacted Brad, and they went over to the crown attorney's office and picked up the warrants.

They then headed with a backup of uniformed officers to the home of Elliott Brown on Jarvis Street.

Elliott answered the door when they arrived, and Tom advised him he was under arrest for drug trafficking and the second-degree murder of the four overdose victims from the heroin laced fentanyl. They read Elliott his rights and turned him over to two of the uniformed officers to take him into custody.

Brad then informed Elliott that they had a search warrant to search his premises.

The uniformed officers took Elliott out to a waiting cruiser and put him in the rear seat. They waited with him in the cruiser while the detectives in conjunction with a CID team entered the home to conduct the search.

Uniformed officers set up a police line around the front of the home based on established protocol which proved to be a wise action.

The neighbors from across the street had gathered in their front lawns watching the activities that were unfolding that Friday morning at the home of the man they knew as Elliott Carson.

The looks of concern and amazement showed on many of their faces as they recalled the tragic events of September 10th just short of five weeks earlier at the Shepherd's home.

Someone had obviously notified the press as reporters and a camera crew arrived shortly thereafter from the London CTV news channel and the London Free Press.

The officer on duty informed the media that the detectives responsible for the scene were inside the home executing a search warrant and the lone occupant was currently in custody but no further details would be available until the detectives in charge completed their search. An official either at the scene or from police headquarters would be holding a press conference at some point after the search is completed, and they may have more to advise.

Tom, Brad, and the CID team were moving carefully through the home looking for any evidence regarding the drug trafficking operation. They were aware that the search warrant did not include any materials that may be connected to the Shepherd girl's murder unless they were reasonably found in plain view as a result of the drug trafficking warrant search.

They completed the bedrooms on the second floor and proceeded to the bedroom, kitchen, dining room, and living room on the main floor without finding anything of significance.

The team moved to the basement and began searching the cupboards and drawers in the cabinets downstairs.

Brad noted that the one cabinet standing against a wooden paneled wall appeared to have several scuff marks on the concrete floor in front of the legs, so the CID team attempted to move the cabinet.

The cupboard moved out easily and behind the cupboard was a small door in the wooden paneling. When the team opened the door, they found a small cubbyhole that was approximately two feet deep and was two feet by three feet in size.

It appeared that the wooden wall paneling concealed a false space and the cubbyhole had been built into that space.

Inside the cubbyhole, they located several brown paper bags containing what appeared to be heroin and fentanyl packages which the CID team removed and field-tested verifying the contents.

They could not verify at the scene if any of these bags contained a mixture of heroin-laced fentanyl but Tom was certain that this evidence would provide the last piece to tie Elliott Brown to the drug trafficking operation and the statements of Mr. Caruthers and Smith would tie him to the murder charges.

The cubbyhole also contained a quantity of cash as well as a small ledger that detailed the drug exchanges between the parties including the exchange listed for September 7th.

Tom was pleased that they had evidence that definitely supported the trafficking and second-degree murder manslaughter charges against Elliott but was frustrated that there was no evidence found to tie him to the Shepherd's homicide which he firmly believed Elliot was responsible for.

Tom asked the CID team to document, collect, and remove the evidence they had found from this initial search, and told the team he planned to continue the search on the following Monday after they had the opportunity to question Elliott Brown.

Tom and Brad exited the home and were greeted by the press representatives requesting a statement for the evening news.

Tom took the lead and made the following statement:

"All we can confirm at this time is that the occupant Mr. Elliott Brown aka Mr. Elliot Carson has been arrested and charged for drug trafficking and for second degree murder related to the four overdose homicide cases that occurred on the weekend on September 7th and 8th in London resulting from the trafficking of heroin laced fentanyl.

"The investigation is ongoing, and an official press conference will be scheduled by the police station public affairs department when there is more information to release."

The reporter for CTV news leaned into Tom and asked:

"Is this investigation tied in any way to the homicide of Deborah Shepherd that occurred on the Monday of September 10th in the home next door to Mr. Brown's?"

"I have no comment on that at this time," Tom responded.

"But it seems very strange that the homicide of the young Shepherd girl happened right after the weekend in question regarding the drug homicides and in the home right next door to Mr. Brown, can you elaborate on that?"

"I have no comment nor am I able to engage in speculation regarding that line of questioning, so I will ask you to kindly wait for the official press conference and news release from the department. Thank you."

Tom turned away from the reporters and headed over to the police cruiser where Mr. Brown sat in the rear seat looking defiant and furious.

"Take Mr. Brown to the station and book him on the trafficking and second-degree murder charges related to the heroin laced fentanyl. Ask the crown attorney to ensure he is held over the weekend in the Elgin Middlesex Detention Facility and we will interview him Monday morning," Tom advised the uniformed officers.

"That way he should have the weekend to stew over his arrest and get a lawyer before we interview him on Monday morning," Tom commented to Brad, "I want him to sweat a little and give his attorney time to fill him in on the full details of his charges since they are so iron clad.

"I just wish there was some way to charge him on the Shepherd's homicide so that the Shepherd family can have some closure since I am convinced he is the culprit."

Tom and Brad returned to the station and finished out their day before heading home for the weekend.

Tom arrived home in time for the six o'clock newscast on CTV and watched his press conference from the scene earlier in the day.

Ann asked him how it was going, and Tom gave her the highlights and his frustration at not being able to wrap up the Shepherd girl's murder.

Ann advised him that the real estate agent had called and that she had three offers on the home from the three couples that had toured the home during this week. The realtor wanted to arrange to come to the house tomorrow morning and have the three buyers' agents present their offers.

"Did she say how the offers looked?" Tom asked.

"Her comment was that one was a full price offer no conditions, one was $5,000 over asking price with some conditions and the other was a $10,000 over asking price with some conditions and a relatively short closing date for occupancy."

Tom considered his wife's comments and could not really believe that the house had offers so quickly and above asking.

"She is coming at 10:00 in the morning and then the buyer's realtors will come one at a time twenty minutes apart to present their offers," Ann continued.

Tom and Ann continued their evening as normal by sharing the evening meal and watching TV so that Tom could de stress from his day. Ann thought to herself that she would be so pleased in just three weeks when Tom would retire from the police force, and all the problems and emotional issues that he faced everyday as part of the job would be over.

At 9:50 on Saturday morning, the realtor agent arrived at the home and discussed with Tom and Ann the procedure for the presentation of the offers.

"I will have the three agents come in separately twenty minutes apart and allow them to go over their clients offer details, etc. You are not to make any statements regarding acceptance of any of the offers but can ask any questions you have regarding the offer specifics. After each one leaves, we will discuss the offer amongst ourselves and then I will have the next agent come in and present their clients offer. Incidentally, we have four offers to present this morning instead of three as a fourth offer was received last night. Any questions before we start?"

"Not really," Tom commented, "We will trust your judgment as this unfolds."

The agent then went outside and came back in with the first presenter.

"Greetings, my name is Harry Black for Re Max realty. I would like to begin by saying that my clients were very impressed with your home and are therefore making an offer for the full asking price. Here is a copy of the offer, Mr. and Mrs. Harvey have a young family and are looking for a 'forever' home to raise their children. The offer has no conditions as they are not selling a current home and have been pre-approved for the amount. Closing date is flexible, but they need to provide a minimum of 60-day notice to their landlord under their lease, so they could close in mid-December. Do you have any questions?"

Tom and Ann looked at their relator and their relator commented, "No, I believe this offer is clear and straight forward."

"Thanks for your presentation," stated the Grants relator, "As you are aware we have four offers that are being presented this morning and I will get back to you shortly. I should mention that some of the other offers are above asking if you want to go back and discuss with your clients."

"Let me talk with the Harveys." Mr. Black responded, and I will advise them. "I will get back to you regarding my discussion if they want the offer to stand as is or if they wish to modify it in any way."

After Mr. Black left Ann, Tom, and their relator discussed the offer which she felt was a good one on its own merits. She then went to get the second presenter.

The second realtor agent came in and presented her offer.

"My name is Cynthia and here is my card. My clients are prepared to purchase your home at a price that is $10,000 over asking based on the following conditions. The Shafters have a home they have on the market for sale and therefore the purchase offer and closing dates are subject to the sale of their home. They feel they will be able to sell their home and will be able to establish a closing within 60 days of the sale of their property."

"As you are aware, my clients have multiple offers to consider," replied the Grants relator, "And as such if they were to accept the Shafter's offer it would be subject to a clause that would require the Shafter's to waive the condition if the sale of their property did not occur within a reasonable time frame."

"What time frame would you be looking at?"

"Let me discuss that with the Grants and advise you after we have reviewed the offers. Thanks for your presentation and I will be back to you."

The realtor left just after which their realtor advised Tom and Ann that although the offer was $10,000 over asking, the conditions made the sale and closing dates uncertain. She advised that they withhold judgment until the other two offers had been considered but that this was not the most desirable offer in her professional opinion.

The third buyer's realtor then came in and proceeded to follow the same process as the other two presenting the written offer to Tom and Ann.

"My clients are offering $5,000 over the asking price. The only condition is the closing date which needs to be 90 days from now placing the closing mid-February as the buyers are relocating from out of province. They have been pre-approved for the mortgage loan and their current home is under contract to close the end of January."

The Grant's realtor discussed the contract in place for the buyer's current home to review conditions on that sale, and the buyer's realtor provided a copy of the sale contract that the buyers had in place.

The Grant's realtor thanked him for the presentation of the offer and advised that she would get back to him after the offers had all been reviewed.

That brought the process to the fourth and final relator's presentation.

She introduced herself and explained that the offer was for the full asking price. Her buyers were first time homebuyers and had been pre-approved for the amount of the offer with their available down payment. Closing date would be January 1st so that they could provide adequate notice to their landlord to vacate the lease.

After the fourth presenter left the Grant's realtor then recapped and reviewed the four offers. Tom and Ann advised that although the one offer was

$10,000 over asking they were not comfortable waiting to see if the buyers are able to sell their home.

Their realtor received a call on her cell phone and answered the call as it was from the first realtor who had presented. After she hung up, she advised Tom and Ann that the first couple had amended their offer and increased the offer to $5,500 over asking.

Tom and Ann discussed all the pros and cons with their realtor and decided to accept the amended offer of the first couple.

The Grant's realtor called back to the buyer's agent and reached agreement on a closing date of December 13th. She advised the realtor to deliver an amended offer to her at 1:00 p.m. signed by the buyers, and she would get the Grants to sign this afternoon.

Tom and Ann discussed further details of the sale process with the relator who then left advising she would call later today and arrange a time for Tom and Ann to sign the purchase agreement.

Tom and Ann spent the balance of the day discussing what had occurred that afternoon, after the relator left with the fully executed sale agreement, Ann called the rental agent at Springbank on the Park and advised they would be taking the apartment as of December 1st.

The leasing agent emailed Ann the finalized lease agreement with the dates filled in for December 1st and everything was finished and in place.

It would take a couple of days for everything to sink in as the major change in their life style had occurred so quickly over a one-week period.

In his mind, Tom realized that he now knew what he would be doing for the first month of his retirement: getting things packed and ready for the move and everything that was involved with the sale of the home they had lived in for most of their married life.

He felt a twinge of apprehensive in how he would describe the decision they had made to the family and to their friends at church the next day. Deep down he knew it was the right move and that everyone would feel the same way; it was just a little unnerving, as it had happened so quickly.

CHAPTER 6:
WEEK THREE

Monday morning October 15th started like every other morning with Tom arriving at the station and filling his coffee cup before he entered his office and settled behind his desk.

It was the same as every Monday except that this week Tom had an even more pronounced realization that his working career was drawing towards its conclusion emphasized by the decisions that he and Ann had made over the weekend to change their home address and life style.

Regarding the upcoming interview with Elliott Brown, the crown attorney had processed the drug trafficking charges and the four counts of second-degree murder against Elliott based on the evidence that he had knowingly provided the heroin-based fentanyl in question. This was being collaborated by the sworn statements of Carruthers and Smith who were testifying that Elliott had 'mixed' the drugs based on the comments Elliott had made to the two of them directly, which made the evidence direct and not hearsay.

Tom was hoping that this could be used as leverage to get Elliott to cut a deal and provide his suppliers farther up the chain.

Tom spent the next hour reviewing the evidence file from the Shepherd's homicide and something caught his attention. The file contained the report from CID regarding the muddy boot print on the back porch and the photo of the print.

He wondered if there was any possibility that the print could be matched to any boots that may be in Elliott's home or the ones he has on in the jail.

It seemed like a long shot but was at least something to consider so Tom called the crown attorney and asked if the search warrant would cover the checking of Elliott's shoes. The crown attorney advised that, just to be safe, he would request an amendment to the warrant to expand the search which would allow for CID to check the boots at Elliott's residence and to check Elliott's current boots.

In their discussions, Tom reviewed the murder charges against Mr. Brown with the crown attorney and the goal of getting Elliott to provide information against those involved in the next level of the trafficking chain. Tom advised that this would likely involve a plea bargain to get Elliott to cooperate.

The crown attorney felt the plan was workable and agreed to meet Tom at the corrections center to expedite the process if they got Mr. Brown to agree to provide the names, details, and testify against the higher-level perpetrators. This could be the chance to bring down a significant portion of a drug trafficking ring.

Any plea bargain reached on the drug trafficking and related homicides from the drug overdoses would have no effect on any evidence or potential charges if Tom could bring in enough evidence to charge Mr. Brown on first-degree murder for the Shepherd girl.

The crown attorney advised he would meet Tom at the detention center at 10:30 this morning and would also get back to Tom on the amended search warrant.

Tom called the CID and told them he was going to wait till after the new search warrant was received before he would have them go back to the Brown's premises and also to arrange to check Elliott's boots at the detention facility against the crime scene photographs.

Tom contacted Brad and arranged to meet him at 10:00 to drive over to the Elgin-Middlesex Detention Centre and formally interview Mr. Brown.

Tom met Brad in the parking area and brought Brad up to date on this morning discussions with the crown attorney as the two of them drove the short distance to the detention center.

After signing in, they were made aware that Mr. Brown had been advised of the upcoming interview and was currently in an interview room conversing with his attorney which worked out well for the detectives.

Tom and Brad met the crown attorney in an observation room next to the interview room while the center staff advised Elliott and his attorney that the detectives were here to interview him. They then brought Tom and Brad to the interview room.

Upon entering, Tom and Brad introduced themselves and advised that they were here to formally interview Mr. Brown on the drug trafficking and four counts of second-degree murder that the crown attorney had charge him with.

Elliott sat across the table and looked as sullen and angry as the last time they had the pleasure of interviewing him after the Shepherd's homicide. His attorney introduced himself, and Tom noted that this time it was not a public defender but a lawyer who he had heard of before who worked for a local criminal defense office in London.

The lawyer started, "I am advising my client not to answer any questions without consulting me first as we will be challenging all the charges based on the evidence. In addition, my client has not yet appeared before the court until this afternoon for a preliminary hearing and we will be requesting bail be set at that time."

Tom thought about the requirements of a preliminary hearing which entailed the crown attorney only being required to convince the judge that there is enough evidence that a judge could find the defendant guilty. In this case, he had no worries that the crown attorney could not show the judge sufficient evidence and then the trial will be ordered and scheduled to take place.

Tom realized that the trial process could and would likely take several months in the superior court of justice unless a plea deal was made between the accused and the crown attorney.

In the cases of Mr. Carruthers and Mr. Smith, Tom understood that the outcome was a plea agreement and that he would therefore not be spending months of his retirement 'advising' on those cases for the crown attorney. In the case of Mr. Brown, a plea deal may be reached for the second-degree murder and trafficking charges if Mr. Brown was willing to plead guilty and cooperate on the drug supply chain. That would extract Tom from that case.

But in all probability if a case can be made for the Shepherd's homicide that case would likely go all the way through the judicial system. That meant that Tom would have to make himself available as the investigating detective to support the crown attorney throughout the trial process as needed. Curtailing certain retirement activities and requiring him and Ann to be more restrained in scheduling any trips or lengthy periods away from home.

"The main information we are interested in from Mr. Brown is any details he can provide regarding the trafficking chain that he is part of. You may challenge the charges all you wish but we have sworn testimonies from his two co-perpetrators that Mr. Brown is not only their main supplier but that he admitted to knowingly and willfully mixing the heroine and the fentanyl that resulted in the four counts of second-degree murder," Tom stated.

"If Mr. Brown is willing to cooperate regarding the drug trafficking ring and provide the names and information on his associates that will lead to their arrests as well as being willing to testify the crown attorney has already authorized us to discuss a potential plea deal."

"Coming in rather early with the discussions of a plea deal since my client has not even been seen by the judge on a preliminary hearing," The lawyer commented.

"We are not worried about the outcome of the preliminary hearing based on the evidence as this is a no brainer, but we are willing to deal based on what Mr. Brown can give us regarding the drug trafficking ring that he is an intricate part of."

"What exactly would my client be looking at?" the lawyer questioned.

"The crown attorney has indicated, that if the information Mr. Brown can provide is valid and actionable, he is willing to reduce the four second degree murder charges down to manslaughter and lump the four into one concurrent sentence and stipulate to a sentencing recommendation of three years."

"What about the trafficking charge?"

"If the information is worthwhile the crown is willing to recommend one year on that count to be served concurrently with the manslaughter sentence."

"Let me discuss with my client and I will let you know."

"The crown attorney is here at the corrections facility and available if we reach agreement in the next 20 minutes otherwise he has indicated that the deal drops off the table and will proceed with the hearing this afternoon and simply allow the process to proceed. I am sure you have advised your client of what the potential outcomes could be if he proceeds through the court system."

Tom and Brad left the room and joined the crown attorney in the observation room as Elliott and his lawyer huddled together in the interview room. The crown attorney advised Tom and Brad that the judge had signed the amended search warrant for Elliott's premises and boots. The warrant had been sent over to CID, and they would proceed to check the shoes in the inmate's personal storage at the detention center this morning and be available to meet the detectives at Mr. Brown's premises at their convenience.

Nearly twenty minutes past before Elliott's lawyer requested that the detectives return to the interview room accompanied by the crown attorney.

"My client is willing to provide the names, addresses, and information regarding the drug trafficking ring based on what we discussed for the plea bargain," he turned to the crown attorney, "We will need the plea bargain in writing before my client provides the information."

"Agreed," the crown attorney responded, "with the provision that the information your client provides is verified and results in chargeable offenses and convictions against the other members of the drug trafficking ring."

"Understood," replied Elliott's attorney.

"I will go and get the agreement written up and meet with you at 2:00 p.m. this afternoon at which time your client will be prepared to meet with the detectives and provide sworn information about the details as we have discussed. I will advise the judge that we are postponing the preliminary hearing till tomorrow due to the fact that we are negotiating a potential plea agreement."

The two attorneys shook hands and then Tom, Brad, and the crown attorney left the interview room.

"I will meet the two of you back here at 2:00 this afternoon," commented the crown attorney.

"Hopefully this information will prove to be worthwhile in regard to the drug trafficking operation and we will continue to quietly keep looking into Elliott's connection to the Shepherd's murder," Tom replied.

The three of them left with Tom and Brad heading back to the police station, stopping for lunch on the way.

During lunch, Tom told Brad all about the weekend activities regarding the sale of his home and the upcoming move. It still felt unreal since it happened so quickly that Tom was having trouble adjusting to the fact in his own mind.

Tom was convinced that Ann, on the other hand, was spending the day getting movers quotes and planning for the transition. She had stated at breakfast that she was calling the rental agent to arrange access to the apartment to take measurements for furniture placement and to arrange for 'upgrades.' The landlord was agreeable that the tenants could make alterations that improved the apartment for their use so long as they understood that any physical changes had to remain when the tenants vacate.

Ann was getting a closet design company to reconfigure the main bedroom walk-in closet shelving, arranging to install pull out cupboard inserts in the drawers in the kitchen and have drapes made to fit the three large windows.

The $5,500 over asking price on the home was being utilized to make the apartment a space that Ann could live in for a long time which was her stated goal.

Tom looked forward to his den, the onsite swimming pool, and exercise room as his key amenities, and he was pleased that Ann was enthused by the transition.

"Happy wife – happy life," Brad commented, "that's the way the saying goes."

At 1:45 p.m., Tom and Brad again entered the Elgin-Middlesex Detention Centre and met with the crown attorney.

The three of them entered the same interview room where Elliott and his lawyer were waiting.

The crown attorney provided a copy of the plea agreement to Elliott's attorney who spent the next fifteen minutes reading it over and explaining it to his client.

"Do you understand the terms and what the agreement entails?" he asked Elliott.

"Sure, I understand. Don't like it but I understand," Elliott replied curtly.

"Your client needs to fully understand that this is all conditional on his providing true and actionable information that will result in charges being laid and that he has agreed to testify against those individuals regarding whom he provides information," the crown attorney reiterated.

"Sure, sure," Elliott snarled, "Just give me a pen and let's get this over with."

The attorneys along with Elliott proceeded to sign the document and the crown attorney provided a copy to Elliott's lawyer.

"I will leave the four of you alone to proceed regarding the provision of the stipulated information. Once the detectives advise that the information provided meets the terms of the plea agreement then I will arrange a court appearance to enter the plea," commented the crown attorney, and after shaking hands with the client's attorney left the interview room.

Tom and Brad turned on a recorder, opened their pads, and settled into chairs for what they perceived would be a long afternoon of questions and preparing written statements.

Elliott began by writing down a flow chart of the drug trafficking structure that he was involved in which proved to be quite intricate.

It listed the names and addresses of other mid-level suppliers in Toronto, Hamilton, Windsor, Kitchener, and surrounding communities. In addition, he listed the name and address of the main supplier located in Toronto who Elliott believed was the importer of the drugs into Ontario. Elliott also stated that he was aware there was a large supply coming into Toronto on Wednesday this week because the mid-level distributors had been advised that there would be shipments being placed into safety deposit boxes Thursday for pickups.

The system that was being used involved the utilization of customer mailboxes in a mail service storefront operation that rented mailboxes and package services to the public in Toronto. This storefront acted as a front and pick up point for the drug ring. The main supplier would bring in the packaged drugs on the Thursday morning before the store opened and place them into the ten boxes that were designated for their operation. The mid-level suppliers would come to the store during the morning on Thursday and pick up their parcels by using their key to access their designated box. They would leave the cash proceeds from the sales during the period since the last pick up inside the box before relocking it

Elliott explained that they paid a set price to the main supplier and then added on the costs for their operation and for their distributors in the various cities. Thursday evening Elliott would break down the larger package into smaller 'baggies' for his street dealers, Pete and John, for them to sell over the next week. On Friday of each week, he would meet with Carruthers and Smith in the park and exchange the 'baggies' for the cash that they had collected the week prior.

Tom felt reluctantly impressed at how simple and yet effective the system was.

Elliott wrote down everything in a formal document and then provided a signed sworn affidavit to the information. Tom and Brad called the crown attorney and recapped to him of what had transpired.

The crown attorney conversed with the attorney for Mr. Brown and advised him that Mr. Brown would be required to agree to stay in the detention center till Friday without the request for the bail hearing in order to allow the police to follow through and verify his statements. If that proved out, then the plea deal would be presented to the judge at a prescheduled preliminary hearing on the Monday of the next week.

The attorney agreed, and Elliott reluctantly went along with the plan.

Tom and Brad took the signed document and then proceeded to the crown attorney's office to finalize before heading back to the station.

"How do we want to handle this?" Brad asked.

"Let's get this to the deputy chief's office as this may be the prime opportunity to take down the whole operation with the exchange arranged to happen Thursday this week. If we can coordinate a multi-department operation, we could get all the mid-level suppliers in one scope, the storefront operation, and the main supplier."

When they arrived at the station, they contacted Deputy Chief Jones and arranged a meeting to provide the information that had been obtained.

After reviewing the recorded and written statement and the details of what would be occurring this Thursday, Deputy Chief Jones stated that he would get in touch with the various police forces involved and arrange a video conference for the next morning. If all the departments and various crown attorneys agreed, they would set up a collaborative sweep operation to grab the mid-level suppliers after they had picked up their supplies and then raid the storefront when the main supplier came in Thursday to collect his funds.

Tom left the deputy chief's office and cleaned up his desk to head home for the evening with his mind focusing on what would be required over the course of this week. For the London department, there would be little activity for the force to be involved in as they had already arrested the mid-level supplier Elliott and his two street dealers.

At supper that evening, Ann asked why Tom was being so quiet and showed concern that maybe he was having second thoughts on the decision to move to the apartment. Tom reassured her that his thoughts were on work and not the move, so Ann proceeded to bring him up to date on her day's activities.

As planned, she had arranged for movers to move them December 1st to the apartment which would allow them time to clean the house and do any touch ups before the actual closing date for the sale. Even though the buyers had bought the home 'as is,' Ann was not going to turn over keys to a house that was not clean and spotless. Again, Tom realized what his November retirement would entail plus the first two weeks of December.

Ann was meeting the representatives from the closet shelving company, the kitchen cupboard drawer company and the drapes company on Thursday afternoon at the apartment to get measurements and pick out drapery fabric. She asked Tom if he wanted to take some time off work on Thursday and meet her at the apartment to go over the costs, materials, and designs.

"No," Tom replied, "I trust your judgment and your taste, so you really don't need me to simply get in the way and possibly muddle up the works."

Tom arrived at the office Tuesday morning and had a message for him and Brad to meet with Deputy Chief Jones in the main conference room at 10 a.m. sharp.

When they arrived the deputy chief, crown attorney, and senior members of the department were in attendance. A video conference call link had been set up for senior police officers from each of the affected jurisdictional departments to attend, and they were waiting for everyone to sign on. Copies of the statement signed by Elliott Brown outlining the drug trafficking operation and what was expected to occur this Thursday had been scanned and emailed to the senior officers of the various municipal police forces involved and the Ontario Provincial Police (OPP).

It appeared the OPP officials had been at the station since the crack of dawn coordinating with London Police Services officials in preparation for this morning's call. In addition, senior officers from Hamilton, Windsor, and Kitchener had driven into the London station that morning in person rather than attending by video conference.

Tom and Brad took seats against the wall on the side of the room and waited for things to happen. Tom observed the conference room had been modified from simply a meeting room to a more functional command center overnight. A bank of phone lines had been placed on a communications desk array along the far wall.

He had been aware of the capability as this room was designed to be utilized as a main communication and command center in the event of a crisis involving the police emergency measures response. In the past this room had functioned as the arterial link between the police mobile emergency response van and various city departments such as fire and ambulance during emergency preparation drills for natural disaster or potential terrorist activity.

Resulting from the 9/11 terror attacks in 2001 when Al Qaeda terrorists had used hijacked commercial airplanes to bring down the twin towers of the World Trade Center in New York City the Canadian federal government had allocated preparation funds to emergency response units across the country. Fortunately, the system had only been activated for smaller natural disasters, transportation and chemical spills, and major fires. The unit had not needed to be activated for major disasters or terrorist threats.

One by one the senior officers from departments in Metropolitan Toronto, Whitby, Peterborough, Barrie, Niagara Falls and St. Catherine's signed on to the video conference call.

After the all-around introductions were made by the attendees listing the police forces they represented, Deputy Chief Jones turned the meeting over to OPP Commissioner Vince Loveday who would be the lead coordinator for the joint operation.

Commissioner Loveday introduced the members of the OPP Organized Crime Enforcement Bureau and Provincial Operations Intelligence Bureau who would be assisting in the coordination of the operation. He then Asked Tom as the lead detective to go through the statement provided by Elliott Brown and re state the description of how the drug trafficking ring was organized.

Tom re quoted what Elliott had stated and written in his statement detailing how the drug trafficking ring was structured. He described how the main supplier in Toronto was the one importing Heroine and Fentanyl, but Elliot was not aware of how the drugs were being brought into the country.

The structure was in place so that the main supplier would not be required to move large quantities but had a network of ten mid-level suppliers in the various cities across southern Ontario. These mid-level suppliers would come to Toronto on a weekly or every two-week basis and pick up a quantity of the drugs depositing cash receipts. In order to do this, the operation had obtained a mailbox store franchise in Toronto that was being used as a front in order to provide a drop point. The ten mid suppliers had keys to specific mailboxes in the storefront and on the designated day, they would simply travel into the city, exchange the cash wrapped in a brown paper parcel for the brown paper wrapped supply of the drugs. Elliott had confirmed that he would then bring his parcel back to London and re package the drugs into smaller quantities which he would then provide to the two individuals who would act as street sellers for the product in London.

The same basic process was being used by the other nine mid-level suppliers and the organization had set up strict geographical boundaries within which each mid supplier would have their street sellers work.

This way the operation could move a significant quantity of drugs over a short period of time, but the operation stayed small enough to operate under the normal radar of the various individual police organizations across southern Ontario.

The lead for the OPP Organized Crime Enforcement Bureau thanked Tom for the recap and asked if there were any questions regarding the mechanics of the operation.

Comments were stated by various members of the newly organized multi-jurisdictional task force regarding the simplicity of the operation.

The OPP lead then outlined the plan for two days from now, Thursday when the exchanges were scheduled to take place in Toronto.

All communications regarding the operation which had been labelled 'Mailbox' for identification purposes would be handled by land line and cell phone calls, no open band police radios would be used to communicate and coordinate during the operation in order to ensure no potential informational leaks.

The communications center would be set up here at London Police Services and Deputy Chief Jones had assigned detectives Tom Grant and Brad Logan as the focal point for all communications to be coordinated through.

The OPP had arranged to set up a surveillance operation on the mailbox storefront utilizing an empty apartment across the street from the mailbox store. Surveillance teams would be in place this afternoon, and they will observe the storefront throughout tomorrow and Thursday. The plan was for the surveillance team to take pictures of the arrival of the main supplier and document activities as well as the arrival of the nine remaining mid-level suppliers.

A designated undercover team would tail each of the nine mid-level suppliers after they pick up their drug supply back to their respective cities and locations. Once the surveillance teams had confirmed the arrival of all of the mid-level suppliers back at their locations then the command would be given and the various department take down teams would mobilize under the direction of their respective OPP coordinators to apprehend the mid-level suppliers with the drugs.

This would be coordinated with the arrival back at the mailbox store of the main supplier to retrieve the funds deposited from the drops.

One potential issue would be the fact that the London mid-supplier would not be arriving at the storefront to pick up his supply. It had been discussed whether it would be better for Elliott Brown to be used to make the pickup, but the decision had been to let that pass. Hopefully the main supplier would assume that something had gone amiss regarding Elliott's pick up and that he could then be caught not only with the cash proceeds but the drugs that were scheduled for the London pickup.

The Provincial Operations Intelligence Bureau representative questioned whether there was any option in this operation to try and locate the method of importation being used to smuggle the drugs into the country either by the main supplier or those possibly higher up in the organization.

After a discussion on the topic, it was determined that there was no feasible method to structure the operation to achieve that goal without risking the take down of the ring.

The hope was that once they had the main supplier in custody then a deep search into his background and contacts may provide some links farther up the operation.

The discussion continued for the next hour with details of how the individual departments would action the various takedowns, how many officers would be involved, how the departments would stage their resources, etc.

Once completed the joint task force broke and agreed to reconvene by conference call at 4:00 p.m. to recap and ensure everyone was in place for their portion of the operation.

The main communications and coordination team, consisting of Tom, Brad, Deputy Chief Jones, OPP Commissioner Loveday, and the two senior officers from the OPP organized crime unit and the Intelligence Bureau agreed to meet back in the communications center at 2:00 p.m. that afternoon to run checks on the phone communication system and prepare for the 4:00 p.m. conference call.

Tom and Brad left and went to grab lunch bringing their food back to Tom's office so that the two of them could discuss the morning's activities in private.

"Have you ever been involved in this type of operation before?" Brad questioned.

"We utilized a task force during the 'Christmas Ornament' serial killing investigation back when I first started as a detective but that was the only major multi-jurisdictional task force that I have been part of," Tom answered. "Other than that the task forces have been internal London Police and Emergency Services activities."

"It's kind of ironic," Tom continued. "I basically started my detective career with the multi-jurisdictional serial killer case and everything that investigation entailed, and I am ending my detective career with a multi-jurisdictional drug trafficking case.

"I still would love to wrap up the Shepherd girl's homicide before I retire so that I don't need to leave that case incomplete for my peace of mind."

"Since we are still convinced that Elliott Brown is the perpetrator in that homicide you have two weeks to work your magic," Brad commented.

Tom simply grunted as his mind was jumping between the two cases and the memory of his first case, the Christmas ornament serial killer. He had been assigned to work under the direction of veteran detective Ed Morgan. Ed had been a legend in the detective department, solving a record number of cases over his forty-four-year career at that time. He had been brisk and would not hesitate to criticize Tom but Tom realized that Ed was only grooming him to be a good detective.

The Christmas ornament case had taken four months to identify the perpetrator involving a multi-task force from Woodstock, London, and St. Thomas where the murders were taking place.

After that case had concluded, Ed advised Tom that he now had his 'feet wet,' and Tom was assigned to another partner. Ed had continued with the department for two more years but he never retired. Ed died of a massive heart attack at his desk in the station on a Tuesday morning.

His mind snapped back to what was going to occur this week and what they may find Friday at the Brown residence when CID executed the amended search warrant. He was hoping everything runs smoothly Thursday and that Friday would see a break in the homicide.

At 2:00 p.m., they gathered back in the communication center and then proceeded to communicate with the designated communication representatives in each of the various departments to verify that all sections of the multi-task force were able to communicate and be coordinated with during the critical activities that would take place Thursday.

4:00 p.m. arrived and all of the players signed on to the conference call. Each respective department detailed their preparations for Thursday for their individual operations. The OPP lead confirmed that the surveillance teams were in place overlooking the storefront and that the undercover details who were assigned to trail the mid-suppliers back to their locations would be mobile and ready at 6:00 a.m. on the morning of the operation in the vicinity around the storefront to discreetly follow the suspects.

The operations center then shut down for the evening, and Tom and Brad confirmed they would be back at 5:00 a.m. on Thursday to man the communications center. Tom knew that tomorrow was going to be a long day as they waited for Thursday to arrive.

Thursday morning just before 5:00, Tom entered the communications room. The OPP lead and a handful of technicians were already there. Coffee and breakfast pastries had been set up and arranged on a table at the far end of the room as a comfort station during the operation. No coffee, drinks, or other materials would be allowed anywhere else in the room except at the comfort station to ensure no unintentional accidents or spills take place.

As Tom poured a cup of coffee, Brad arrived and joined him.

The technicians were checking the phone lines and the video conference connection which would be kept live throughout the day as a means of communication with the various department command posts.

Deputy Chief Jones arrived at 5:15 as Tom and Brad relocated to the phone line desk to be prepared for any activity.

At 6:30, the first call came into the communication center from the surveillance team located across from the storefront. The main supplier had arrived and parked out front entering the store with a key. He had carried two large duffel bags into the store.

The surveillance team was taking photos of the activity and noted that the suspect had proceeded to turn on the lights in the back section of the store behind the mailbox wall. It was assumed that he would be placing the individual packages of drugs into the individual mailboxes designated for the mid-level suppliers.

Shortly thereafter the individual had turned off the lights, left the store, and locked the front door without taking the duffel bags.

The next call came in at 8:00 a.m. from the surveillance team. The store clerk had arrived and proceeded to open the storefront for normal business hours. The clerk was in his mid-twenties and was wearing a mailbox store shirt and ball cap.

9:30 the first mid-level supplier arrived at the store and was photographed by the surveillance team opening a mailbox and removing a brown paper wrapped package exchanging it for a smaller brown package. He talked with the clerk for a few minutes and then left. The team identified him as the Toronto mid-level supplier identified in Elliott Brown's statement and had notified the respective officer who would tail him as this individual had arrived on foot and was utilizing the Toronto Transit System.

One by one the other mid-level suppliers arrived individually between 9:30 and 11:00 a.m. each following the same procedure and as each one left the storefront designated observation team members took up discrete shadowing positions to tail them back to their respective cities.

By 2:00 p.m., all of the various city police departments had checked in that their mid-level suppliers had arrived back at their various locations and the take down teams were ready to move on command.

At 2:00 p.m., the main supplier reappeared at the storefront and after conversing with the store clerk went behind the mailbox wall. He reappeared shortly with one of the duffel bags that contained material presumed to be the cash from the drops.

The surveillance team observed him in discussion with the clerk, and they then went over to one of the mailboxes and opened it. Inside, they could see the larger brown paper parcel which was likely the unretrieved supply for Elliott Brown in London.

The main supplier took out a cell phone from under the storefront counter and proceeded to attempt to make a call which was apparently not answered. He then made a second call and conversed with the recipient for the next five minutes. The surveillance team assumed that this was likely a burner phone and untraceable.

The operations commander then advised the storefront take down team to move on the main supplier and store clerk and to ensure they retrieved the burner phone before it could be erased as the last call may prove to be a lead to someone else in the operation.

As the storefront team moved in for the arrest, Tom and Brad contacted and advised the operational leads to mobilize and move in on the other nine locations.

One by one over the next thirty minutes, the team leads confirmed the successful apprehension and arrest of the main supplier and clerk in the storefront as well as the mid-level suppliers.

By the time the 6 o'clock news aired, the OPP commissioner had conducted a news conference detailing the take down of a major southern Ontario drug ring that had been organized with a joint task force composed of the various police departments and OPP. He praised the quick actions and cooperation of the various city police forces elaborating on the fact that this operation had succeeded in the removal of a significant supply of heroin and fentanyl off the streets in various cities across the province.

Deputy Chief Jones and the London Police Force were attributed for being the major player in obtaining the information and breaking the drug ring and the commissioner went on to specifically thank detectives Tom Grant and Brad Logan for their exemplary work on this case.

Tom cringed as he watched the news broadcast that evening and considered the comments and joking remarks that he was going to be subject to in the coming days at the station and at home from his family.

As expected, Tom's phone rang at 6:30 with a call from his eldest son and the commentary on 'Super Dad' began.

The next morning when Tom entered the station, his coffee cup proclaiming his upcoming retirement there was a note taped to the front with a picture of superman and the heading 'Super COP.'

He removed the note and proceeded with his cup of coffee to his office which was adorned with a large note on the door proclaiming the office of 'Super Cop,' 'able to leap tall buildings at a single bound…' Inside the office there were various notes and acclamations of his prowess left by individuals in the early hours.

Tom removed all the paraphernalia and proceed to try and concentrate on his day's activities.

At 10:00 a.m. that morning, Tom went to the courthouse to witness the arraignment and sentencing of Elliott Brown in accordance with his plea agreement. Pete Carruthers and John Smith had been arraigned early in the week. Their public defenders along with the crown and attorney had entered their pleas of guilty. The crown had presented the judge with the plea bargain agreements which had been accepted and executed. They were now waiting for sentencing based on the recommendations of the crown attorney contained in the plea agreement.

In Elliott's case, he appeared with his defense attorney and the crown attorney and pleaded guilty. The crown entered the plea agreement which also included the sentencing recommendations that they had negotiated. The judge asked a few questions and then signed the plea agreement turning Elliott over to the court officer to immediately begin his sentence.

Elliott's attorney requested bail which was denied, and the judge advised Elliot and his attorney that since the home Mr. Brown lived in was rented, he could handle making the arrangements for the removal of his belongings etc. from the prison and did not need to be released to handle his affairs.

The whole process was concluded in twenty minutes and Tom watched as Elliott was escorted out of the courtroom by the bailiff.

Tom went back to the station and contacted CID to arrange for them to meet them at the Brown house at 2:00 p.m. that afternoon to execute the new search warrant.

Tom and Brad had decided to not wait till Monday but proceed today since everything regarding the drug ring take down was concluded. In addition, they wanted to ensure that they were ahead of any arrangements Elliott might make to remove items from the house per the judge's statement.

They also requested that the CID team go to the Elgin-Middlesex Detention Centre and retrieve Mr. Brown's shoes held in the inmate storage lockers that he had been wearing when he was arrested and serve the amended search warrant on Elliott.

In order to expedite the process, Tom scanned and emailed a copy of the amended search warrant that listed Mr. Brown's shoes, boots, and other related personal property as covered by the warrant to CID.

He then contacted the landlord who owned the property and advised him that as Elliott Brown was incarcerated they would need access to the premises to exercise a search warrant that afternoon.

The landlord asked what the status was on Mr. Carson i.e. Brown and when he would be getting his items removed. He also asked to know when the police would release to him the property, so he could make arrangements to clean up and re-rent the home.

Tom advised him that at this point it was still an active crime scene but in all likelihood the police would be able to release the property in the near future. In addition, he advised the landlord the basics of what had transpired at the court hearing and that the judge had ordered Mr. Brown to make arrangements to remove his belongings as soon as the property is released from the police investigation.

"We will provide you with the name and contact number of Mr. Brown's attorney when you meet us at the property this afternoon at 2:00 p.m."

Tom and Brad then decided to grab lunch before proceeding to the Brown residence on Jarvis Street.

They arrived just before two, and the landlord was waiting outside the property in his vehicle when they pulled up. He exited his car and came across the street to meet Tom and Brad.

Tom introduced himself and Brad and showed the landlord the search warrant.

"We appreciate your assistance by coming and bringing your key so that we can access the house," Tom commented.

"Can I go inside and take a look at the home's condition?" he asked.

"Sorry but no one is allowed in till after the scene has been released. Here is the card with the phone number and name of Mr. Brown's attorney so you can contact him regarding what arrangements Mr. Brown is making to remove his belongings."

"It's really shook me to my core," the landlord remarked. "He seemed like a normal individual, and he had identification and references under the name of Elliott Carson when he rented the place. Always paid his rent promptly and never had any complaints or concerns during the time he lived here.

"And now finding out that was not his name and that he was trafficking drugs out of my property has shook me badly. Not sure how I feel about continuing to rent the property after this and the publicity associated with the young girl next door being murdered."

Tom again thanked him for his cooperation and told him they would contact him after they were finished and arrange for a uniformed officer to return his key.

After the landlord left, Tom and Brad entered the house along with the CID personnel who had arrived during the exchange with the landlord.

"First thing I need is for you to find every shoe or boot in the house and then take them back to your office for comparison against the boot print that was collected in evidence from the scene at the Shepherd's homicide."

CID went to work searching the house for footwear, and Tom accompanied Brad to do another visual search of the premises. Everything looked the same as it had last time they had been here.

In the basement, the open cubbyhole was visible where they had located the drugs and cash.

Tom was standing in the center of the room staring at a wall covered with hanging tools.

"What are you thinking?" Brad asked.

"The tools, Elliott did not seem to be the handy man type and everything is hung in its place except the one empty spot on the wall."

The two detectives went over to the wall and noticed that the tools were all dust covered and showed no signs of being taken off their racks except the one empty spot.

In looking around the room, they noticed a small crow bar standing against the wall beside the leg of the tool bench.

Tom called the CID lead to come down into the basement and to document the tools and tool rack after which they bagged the crow bar and took it with them for further inspection.

With everything completed, Tom and Brad locked up the premises after CID left and decided to call it a week after they returned to the station to deposit the key, etc. in Tom's desk.

CHAPTER 7:
WEEK TWO

Tom dressed as usual after shaving and showering and realized that a week from this Friday he would be retired. The deadline seemed to be coming faster and faster as the days past, and he knew that this week would be the last week he could dedicate time to work on his final 'unsolved' case of Elliott Brown and the Debbie Shepherd homicide.

Human resources had scheduled meetings and interviews all next week during his final week on the force to finalize paperwork and wrap up files.

Tom was convinced of Elliott's guilt in Debbie's murder; he just needed time to tie up the loose ends and make the case.

He arrived at the office and retrieved his routine cup of coffee before heading to his desk.

The deputy chief called him around 9:00 a.m. to reiterate his appreciation on the outstanding work that Tom and Brad had accomplished on the Brown trafficking case and the resulting arrests.

The press was re-airing the news release and had been calling consistently to get any further information on the operation. The press had latched onto the 'Mailbox' title that had been used to identify the joint task force and were having a field day with the story.

Tom was just pleased that for once the police agencies were being complimented for doing a great job since far too often the press did not broadcast that type of opinion. Looking for alleged police misconduct or inaction was generally what the press was searching for, as it sold newspaper and generated greater followers on newscasts and social media.

10:30, Pete Sloan from the forensics identification unit called Tom. He advised him that they had found a match to the muddy boot print on the back steps of the Shepherds' home with the boots that Elliott Brown had been wearing when he had been arrested.

In addition, they had found dried blood on the crow bar that matched the Shepherd girl's blood and the shape of the curved portion of the crow bar matched the shape and size of the wound on Debbie Shepherd's head.

Tom thanked Pete and asked that he get the reports over to him as quickly as possible.

He sat back and heaved a big sigh of relief before he called Brad and brought him up to speed.

The final call he made was to the crown attorney and told him what had been found. The crown attorney set an appointment for 2:00 p.m. that afternoon for Tom and Brad to come to his office and bring all the evidence and documents on the Shepherd's homicide.

Tom and Brad sat in Tom's office and waited for the reports from Pete Sloan to arrive during which time they made a call to the deputy chief to apprise him of the situation as well.

"Great work to both of you," Deputy Chief Jones stated, "It's wonderful Tom that you are going out with a clean slate and no unsolved cases to make you feel any regret."

The reports from forensics CID arrived at 11:30. After a quick review, Tom and Brad decided to collect the file and grab lunch before heading over to the crown attorney's office.

The crown attorney had Tom and Brad go over the events that had lead up to identifying Elliott as the murderer as well as the evidence that had been collected. The crown then spent some time reading through the CID reports and reviewing the search warrant to ensure all the proper procedures had been followed.

"I don't see anything here that will give a defense attorney any leverage to object to the process that was followed," he stated.

"Looks pretty air tight so my plan is to have Mr. Brown transferred from Elgin-Middlesex Detention Centre to central processing so we can formally lay the first-degree murder charge against him. I will advise his lawyer and make the arrangements for tomorrow morning."

Tom and Brad thanked the crown attorney and prepared to leave having completed officially transferring the reports etc. to the crown. It was his job to take it from here.

"By the way Tom, congratulations and good luck on your upcoming retirement. Unfortunately, this trial is likely to drag on for several months, and we will need you to be available to consult on the case and be prepared to testify as one of the investigating officers. I will try to keep you out of the day to day process by using Brad but there will be some time required," the crown advised.

"No problem," Tom replied, "I have no plans to go on any extended vacations in the foreseeable future so I will be around and available as needed."

After they had finished the meeting, Tom and Brad headed back to the station to wrap up their files for the day.

"What are you planning on doing for the balance of the week now that everything else is complete?" Brad asked.

"I've been told that I will now be desk bound and that I am not to take on any new cases which means you are now basically on your own and the department will provide you a new partner."

"For my part, I want to express my appreciation and let you know how much I have learned working with you these past several months. Not sure who they will partner me up with, but I will always remember what you showed me. Thanks again," Brad commented.

The two men shook hands, and Tom watched as Brad walked out of his office for the last time as his partner.

A feeling of nostalgia started to overcome Tom, and he knew it was time to go home and let things simmer in his mind.

He now had nine more days of 'work' before he officially left but for some odd reason this evening felt like he was walking out for the last time as a detective. It was almost like a tangible change was taking place.

At home, he discussed what had happened with Ann and how he was suddenly feeling, and Ann remarked that she had been walking around the house thinking about the move and the upcoming pack with the movers and she too was feeling that things had already changed.

The two of them discussed together the upcoming life changes and what was likely lying ahead.

Detective Tom Grant went into the kitchen to make a pot of tea with the full understanding that he had concluded his career even though he would not be officially finished till a week from Friday.

THE END.

The Case of the Deadly Seance